P9-ELV-886

invisible girl

Mary Hanlon Stone

invisible girl

philomel books
An imprint of Penguin Group (USA) Inc.

To my home team: my parents, Arthur and Therese,
and my guys, Richie, Jack, and Keith

PHILOMEL BOOKS
A division of Penguin Young Readers Group. Published by The Penguin Group. Penguin Group (USA) Inc., 375 Hudson Street, New York, NY 10014, U.S.A. Penguin Group (Canada), 90 Eglinton Avenue East, Suite 700, Toronto, Ontario M4P 2Y3, Canada (a division of Pearson Penguin Canada Inc.). Penguin Books Ltd, 80 Strand, London WC2R 0RL, England. Penguin Ireland, 25 St. Stephen's Green, Dublin 2, Ireland (a division of Penguin Books Ltd). Penguin Group (Australia), 250 Camberwell Road, Camberwell, Victoria 3124, Australia (a division of Pearson Australia Group Pty Ltd). Penguin Books India Pvt Ltd, 11 Community Centre, Panchsheel Park, New Delhi—110 017, India. Penguin Group (NZ), 67 Apollo Drive, Rosedale, North Shore 0632, New Zealand (a division of Pearson New Zealand Ltd). Penguin Books (South Africa) (Pty) Ltd, 24 Sturdee Avenue, Rosebank, Johannesburg 2196, South Africa. Penguin Books Ltd, Registered Offices: 80 Strand, London WC2R 0RL, England.

Published simultaneously in Canada.
Printed in the United States of America.

Design by Richard Amari.
Text set in Electra LH.

Library of Congress Cataloging-in-Publication Data
Stone, Mary Hanlon. Invisible girl / Mary Hanlon Stone. p. cm. Summary: Fourteen-year-old Stephanie, whisked from Boston to Encino, California, to stay with family friends after her abusive, alcoholic mother abandons her, tries desperately to fit in with her "cousin's" popular group even as she sees how much easier it would be to remain invisible. [1. Interpersonal relations—Fiction. 2. Self-esteem—Fiction. 3. Popularity—Fiction. 4. Family problems—Fiction. 5. Child abuse—Fiction. 6. Muslims—Fiction. 7. Encino (Los Angeles, Calif.)—Fiction.] I. Title.
PZ7.S877942Inv 2010 [Fic]—dc22 2009027255

ISBN 978-0-399-25249-5
1 3 5 7 9 10 8 6 4 2

ACKNOWLEDGMENTS

Special thanks to so many people, beginning with the extraordinary Michael Green, who had the vision for this book, the kindness and patience to guide me along the journey, and the ability to send the funniest e-mails at the perfect time. To Claire Gerus, phenomenal agent and soul sister. You are magical. To Tamra Tuller for all her help. To my sibs, who are always there for me: Colleen Hanlon, savior and sage; Arthur Hanlon, muse musician; John, D.B., Kevin and Noreen, the rest of the home team. Thanks to Alexandra Dew, intrepid teen advisor, and the Stone girls, Tamara, Tali and Carly, for answering weird and random questions. To Lori Wagner for refusing to let me shove the book under my bed. Love you, Dub. To Robin Sax for generously introducing me to Claire. Thanks, Lobna Abdelaziz and Dr. Khaled Abou El Fadl. And, of course, to Richie, the most wonderful man I know, and my beautiful boys, Jack and Cubba.

invisible girl

CHAPTER ONE

Gross. It stinks in here. Like somebody's wet dog.

I look up from my nest of coats on the closet floor and smack the flashlight against my hand hard. I hate it when it does this. When the beam of light flickers like it's about to go out. The batteries aren't even that old. I slap it against my leg even harder this time. The flashlight's lucky it can't bruise, no matter how many times I whack it. I wonder what it would be like not to bruise, no matter how many times I get hit.

I smack the flashlight one last time and the beam finally steadies. I focus it back on the book in my lap and a drop of water falls on my head. I reach up to touch one of my mother's sweaters. It's soaking wet from the rain that's been pouring down outside for three days. No wonder it stinks in here. I want to open the door and toss out the sweater, but can you imagine what would happen if I were discovered? In here? Like this?

Not that I had a choice. The signs were everywhere. I felt fear rip through my body before my brain even registered "danger." My body works faster than my mind. My heart started pounding, my legs started running and deep inside me, my cells screamed, *Noooooooo*. Another part of my body reacted too. I wet my pants. I wet as I ran, like I was three instead of fourteen.

But that's how it feels when this happens. Like I'm smaller and younger than I am. Like I'm nothing.

When I was finally safe in the closet, I had to peel off my pants and underwear. I rolled them into a little ball and shoved them behind the fishing stuff. I threw a windbreaker over my naked butt. It's slippery and makes me cold even though it's hot outside and the rain is like steam.

I run my fingers over the edge of my book. At least I have that. I always keep one waiting with the flashlight, behind the fishing poles and tackle box. I used to keep apples in here too, but then one day I came into the closet and found bugs all over them. Bugs with hard backs and short fat legs, the kind that, when I was a little kid, I thought could be the tanks in a bug war.

I point the flashlight at my Nancy Drew mystery. This is the only place I read Nancy Drews. Normally, I'm way too old for them. I mean, I read all forty-seven of them when I was ten, more than four years ago. I just keep a couple handy in the closet for when things get really scary. They help calm my mind when it catches up to my body and starts to think too much about where I'll be hit next. And if I'll have marks that I'll have to hide at school.

In the closet, I read them over and over, even though I know what's going to happen.

I start reading and I forget about my naked butt and the slippery windbreaker. By now the voices have grown loud. I have to bite on my knuckle to help me concentrate. Sometimes, I bite down so hard, it bleeds. I usually don't even notice the blood until they've gone, when I open the closet door and see things smashed.

I have the knuckle of my right pinkie finger in my mouth now. It's the only one that doesn't have a scab yet. Something smashes against the wall in the kitchen and I squeeze my eyes shut to clear it from my head. I know it was a glass that smashed because it sounded high-pitched, like a woman's scream. When a book is thrown, I hear a dull thud. High heels make sharp, scratching sounds like desperate rats trying to dig into the walls.

I grind into the pinkie knuckle to keep concentrating. In my book, Nancy Drew tries to grab her attacker and a sack is pulled over her head. She tears frantically at the cord around her neck.

I turn the page. Nancy's still struggling. She knows that in a moment she'll black out. She pulls harder on the cord. I put my hands up to my neck to help her.

Something bangs in our kitchen like angry thunder. My head jerks even though I'm trying to read and not hear anything. Footsteps storm into the living room and stop inches away from my sanctuary. *Sanctuary* is one of my old Warrior Words.

I curl into a ball and slide my dad's raincoat over my head so that I'm in a little tent. I keep the flashlight on my book and read the note to Nancy Drew demanding that she give up the Spider Sapphire case.

Something heavy slams against the closet door, which then flies open. My hand shakes as I turn off the flashlight. I try to frame what's happening as if I'm reading about Nancy. *Someone opened her sanctuary!*

It doesn't work. I can smell the whiskey. My throat pitches forward like I'm going to throw up. I taste vomit in my mouth, but I clench my teeth so that it goes back down.

I shut my eyes into hard slits and wait for my words. Nothing happens yet. The whiskey smell is overwhelming. I push on my tightly shut eyes. Then, there's a trembling in the top of my head and a rumbling as my Warrior Words start to tumble down. They come in to save the day when I'm forced to stop reading the Nancy Drews.

Splendiferous bursts in a brilliant rainbow in the middle of my brain, and I have a second of calm. Then there's a hard yank on the raincoat covering me. My word vanishes. My mother stands in front of me like a beautiful, angry witch. She's wearing a sparkly red dress that's dipped low in front so that you can see half her boobs. She and my dad had been at a late afternoon wedding. Her lips are also red, perfect ruby curves except where they're smeared on one side, making her upper left corner look like someone botched an operation.

"What do you think you're doing in here?" my mother says to me, half falling into the upside-down hedge of jackets.

I don't want to see her face. I squeeze myself even smaller so that maybe she'll remember how unimportant I am and be distracted by something else. I sneak my arms to the sides of my head, where they cross over each other on top. I've learned to protect my head.

She laughs, rasping and high, like a witch. I peek at her face to see how much time I have. Her long, black hair is done up in a shiny bun like a queen's. Her hands are on her movie-star waist. For a moment she's a painting: *Beautiful, Angry Woman.*

Her beauty is her power source. People can't take their eyes off of her. The construction workers always whistle at her, and once an old businessman with a red-veined nose said, "Hubba, hubba." Even our priest stares at her in church.

"I thought I told you to clean your room," she hisses at me.

She's lowered her head to say this to me. Her breath comes in fat clouds of whiskey. They puff around my head. Her eyes are red and loose like they can't hold everything in their view at one time.

I dig up a word and put it over her face so I don't have to see her witch anger. *Undulate* glides over her cheeks and across her nose in a silvery splash. A school of fish shoots over the rapids of her forehead.

There's no point in telling her that my room is clean.

My father comes up behind her. His face is white and tired. "Just sleep it off," he says in his nervous voice. "You need to lie down."

He's perfectly sober. He always is around her. He's afraid of all her bottles. The bottles we find in the broom closet, the bathroom cabinet and the clothes hamper.

My mother turns and looks at him. Her mascara rings both eyes. Raccoon Mama. Her voice is an ashtray scraping on concrete. "You are so pathetic. Have I told you how pathetic you are?"

She's pure witch now, no queen. Her mouth is mean and her cheeks bunch up as if even the nerves under them are angry. She turns back to me. Heat pumps into my face. I pray nothing will get broken this time.

"Get up," she spits, and her eyes pierce into me like knives.

I stand slowly and keep my eyes on her shoes. I'm holding the raincoat around my waist and hoping she won't notice it.

"Hang up the coat," she says, then kicks at my nest on the closet floor with the point of her sparkly red high heel. "What the hell kind of mess is this?"

I mumble, "I don't know." I start to edge away from the closet. It's not that far to the stairs. I take one tiny side step but keep looking down. She grabs the coat and jerks it off of me. I feel air on my naked privates.

"What were you doing in there?" she screams.

Shame blisters my face. I look at my dad. His leaky eyes are stuck on my privates with the new dusting of pubic hair, the promise of my period yet to come. "Jesus Christ," he says.

I don't even have time to say anything. She's already hitting me, mostly on my head but also on my shoulders and back. Even though my privates are exposed, I'm glad I don't have to hold up the raincoat anymore because now I can use my arms to cover my head.

She hits harder and harder. Her arms are long, with hard knots for biceps. I close my eyes and a trusty word shimmers like an oasis through sweltering heat in the middle of my brain. I drop to my knees and watch *antidisestablishmentarianism* rise into droplets of glittering diamonds. I'm barely aware of the noise of her slaps and the sharp clink of her bracelets hitting each other when she swings her fist.

When there's a sharp kick in my back, I fall forward. Pain bursts along my side and my word melts away because my breath is coming out so hard and steamy, it couldn't stand the heat.

I open my eyes. My mother's eyes pour into mine, but they're not angry anymore. They look more shocked, like she can't believe that there's a thin stream of blood dripping from the corner of my mouth. She drops to her knees and pulls my head against her chest. "Why do you make me do this?" she whispers. "Why? Why?"

I smell her perfume and know I'm not supposed to answer this question. She starts rocking me and calling me "poor baby."

I feel the pressure in my head and I know I hate her, but I love her stroking my back right now and I'm too dizzy to know how to think about anything.

Sometimes, after she's been at me, I think about killing her. But then, later, she comes into my room, washes my cuts and brushes my hair. She cries and tells me how much she loves me. Sometimes she sleeps in my bed with me, pressing me against her chest, and I sleep in a cloud of warm skin and safety.

I try to pretend I'm in that cloud now, but pain keeps jerking from my back and globs of hate rise like pus in my heart. Then she puts her lips to my ear and starts singing something in a normal mom's voice. My hate globs burst into pure air. I feel an electric current of need running from her bursting breasts to my baby ones, like she knows all the woman secrets of periods and bras and that I won't if she's not with me.

I melt against her.

She puts a last kiss on my cheek and stands. I notice for the first time that there is a suitcase near the door. My face gets hot again but it's a different kind of heat, one that starts in my stomach and feels like I ate old food that's now burning up inside me.

I look at my dad. He looks away fast because he's leaking all over. Invisible water pours out of him, and I wonder if I blew on him, would he just fall over. I know there's nothing to get from him but I say, "Da-ad?"

He moves slowly out of the daze where he hides whenever I'm being beaten. His pale hand with the hairy knuckles reaches out for my mom's arm, but she moves away roughly and the hand falls through the air down to his side empty.

My mother walks to the door and picks up the suitcase. She looks at me. Her eyes are less runny now, as if she can actually see stuff outside her body. I give her my freezing stare like I do on the days when she forgets to pick me up from school and I walk the three miles home rather than letting the nuns know that she isn't coming again. Usually when I do this, if she's not so drunk that she's hitting me, she cries until her eyes are red and she has to use ice on them. Today she doesn't even notice my stare.

I keep it up anyway. I want to stay tough and show her I'm really, really furious, but she isn't even looking at me anymore. She's walked back over to the closet and is flicking through the coats and sweaters. She grabs a couple and lays them over her arm. Then she turns toward the door again.

I notice a run in her black pantyhose right below the back of her knee. Her skin, normally dark, looks bright white where it presses between the black threads.

I plan on hating her forever, then "Don't go" pours out of me from somewhere behind my stomach, somewhere I didn't know about. Before I know it, tears burst. I lurch on my knees and grab her around the waist. The material of her dress is satiny, and I have to hold on hard. Her chain belt is sharp against my face.

"Mom, don't go," I say in a whisper. "I promise I won't take your bottles anymore." My voice sounds wet as if the rain outside has gotten into my throat.

I figure she's had it with me for the bottles. When I'm really mad at her, I scour her hiding places and take the amber containers into the alley and throw them into the dumpster. I like to do this on Mondays after the dumpsters are emptied so they can shatter against the bottom.

My mother's hands claw at mine, trying to pull me off of her. I grunt as I hold on. My hands are dark like hers, Italian hands, not Irish like my dad's. Our fingers are shaped exactly the same except hers end in sharp red nails. Her bangles slam against each other. Then one nail digs into me so hard, I lose my grip.

"Ow," I yelp. Blood rises quickly on the cut as if I had too much in my body in the first place and some was dying to get out.

I look up. She's staring over my head toward the door. I sob and hiccup at the same time. "Mommy, don't leave me" flies out. I haven't called her "Mommy" since I was five.

She kneels down in front of me and pushes her forehead against mine. For a second, she's the queen who comes in my bedroom and brushes my hair that's just like hers. She looks like she's about to tell me something really important when a car beeps outside.

She puts her hands on the floor and makes a small grunt as she starts to get up. I stare hard to direct her eyes back into mine so she can tell me the something important, but she's already standing up with her eyes trained over my head.

The car outside beeps again and she kisses my cheek with a vague swipe of lips like she's already out the door and her lips are running behind her. I can feel the red smudge on my skin. I can smell the whiskey mixed with her perfume. She turns and walks to the door. Her steps are wobbly. My father reaches out and this time grabs her arm. She swings her fist at him. "Don't touch me, *Senator.*"

My father sags back like a bag of flour someone punched.

The car beeps again and she hurries down the front porch steps, almost tripping on the broken one at the bottom. She holds her hand over her head as if it could protect her from the pounding drops. I crawl to the door because it doesn't occur to me to stand up and walk. A big man gets out of the driver's seat and opens her door for her, then tosses her suitcase into the backseat.

My dad watches with me. I want to smack some courage in him to go get her, but I'm afraid if I turn my head to look at him, she'll be gone. Stupidly, I try to think of the right

Warrior Word, as if there were one that could freeze her in her tracks so we could carry her back in, but nothing pops into my head.

She trips on something and her foot turns in the little cage of its high-heel shoe. She stumbles and falls into the passenger seat and slams the door. She doesn't look back at me as the car speeds away, red lights winking through a wall of rain.

I don't even realize that I've stood up in our doorway with no pants or underpants on until some kids whip down the streets on their bikes and yell, "Beeeaver," then laugh as their tires send up white sprays of water, sparkling under the streetlights.

CHAPTER TWO

Everyone is over. Deep voices rumble. Kitchen chairs scrape battered tile. I'm upstairs with my chin resting on the clothing chute. Thank God all of my dad's brothers are loud. Especially when they're drinking. Otherwise it'd be impossible to pick out the words from the big male thunder.

I close my eyes to hear better. My dad's voice sounds higher than his brothers', as if he really wasn't one of them but a stranger, weaned from his mother too early and deprived of vital nutrients. He's saying, "Not even a phone call." Then he tells them about what time she left last night and what the guy in the car looked like.

I know he won't tell them that she squeezed her eyes half shut like an eel and called him "Senator." He couldn't possibly explain that to his broad-shouldered, thick-necked brothers, whose wives bring them beers during football games.

I could go down and tell them though. I know all about it. On queen nights when she brushed my hair she'd tell me that we were all going to end up in the White House. Since my dad's Irish, he'd be like John F. Kennedy, who was the president way back in the 1960s. My dad's going to finish law school, get into local politics, then win all the national races until finally, he runs for president. She's going to be the first lady and have magazines write about what she wears. She says that the only difference between her and Jackie O., who was John F. Kennedy's fancy wife, is that she's Italian rather than French.

I've read all her Kennedy books. When I was younger, we used to pretend we were Kennedys and have conversations with them. My mom knew all their nicknames. When she was tired drunk instead of mean drunk, she talked about redoing rooms in the White House and what type of china she would pick out.

My dad says one more thing but it's blurred, like the words got smudged by his tonsils on the way out. No one says anything for a minute, and then my uncle Pat clears his throat. He's used to making decisions and speaking at meetings. He's a union rep. There are seven boys in my dad's family, all of them still in Boston and all of them, except my dad, working in construction.

My uncle Pat starts talking in low but urgent tones like he's one of the nuns trying to get a nervous kid to stand up and go out on stage for a spelling bee. I hear "family," "time," and "Michael's for a while." I don't know who Michael is.

My uncle Pat has five kids. All my uncles have at least four. My dad is the youngest and he and my mom just have me. My uncle Pat speaks louder and tells my dad to finish law school and get on with his life, that she'll come back.

I cross my fingers. I have secret fantasies I'd never admit to anyone. They started when I was ten and I'm too old for them now, but I keep them anyway, like a nightgown that's become way too short but it's so soft, you wear it. I desperately want my dad to finish law school so he won't be blank anymore and he'll be like Nancy Drew's father, Carson Drew, the distinguished lawyer who solves cases with Nancy's help. Then, I'd get to come into his office, look over important papers and say with a smile and a small shake of my head, "Looks like we've got another one, Dad."

Being like Nancy Drew seems more perfect now than ever. Nancy's mother died when she was three. My mother has left us. It will just be me working with my dad, up against evil-looking thugs with tattoos or normal-looking businessmen who secretly run high school slavery rings. I'll have a housekeeper like Nancy's housekeeper, Hanna Gruen, who will worry about me when I'm not home on time and cluck over my missed meals and going without my raincoat.

Then, if my mom comes back and my dad wants to be president after we've solved around a hundred cases, that will be okay too. I know for a fact that Jackie O. wasn't a drinker, because how could you be passed out or hitting people with all those reporters hanging around the White House?

The image is ruined when I hear something like a choking sound. I lean my head a little farther down. Now it's a gasping. I open my mouth in concentration and my gum slips out and plummets down the chute into the laundry room. I wish I had a sister I could laugh with about the gum.

I strain my ears. Bottles clack. A throat clears. My uncle Kevin says, "Jesus Christ, Liam, buck up." There's another gasp and something cold grows under my skin. My father is crying.

I jerk my head up and bang it on the top of the chute. How can he be crying when he has to get his butt in gear and finish law school?

My mother's face pops into my head, and hate and guilt twist over each other like snakes fighting. Maybe I shouldn't have wished for a Hanna Gruen housekeeper. Maybe my mom thinks I don't want her anymore. Maybe I really don't.

Of course I do. I just want her fixed, so she doesn't hit me anymore. Once, she didn't drink for three whole months, and we made cookies together and did our nails and she brushed my hair and made lots of plans for the White House, where I could talk on the news about what kind of dog we were going to get.

Why isn't my dad going out and getting her? What's wrong with him?

Furious, I run down the stairs and into the kitchen. My father has his head on his crossed arms on the table. My uncle Sean, the oldest brother, has his hand on my dad's shoulder. The other uncles are either still sitting at the table or leaning against the counter. A couple of them hold cigarettes, and the air is familiar with beer and smoke.

I open my mouth to demand that my father go out and get my mother and fix everything. The word *Dad* comes out, but the rest dries up in my mouth when he looks up at me with eyes that sink into his head. I see the stray cat with the torn ear that just kept slinking down when I tried to pet him.

I stumble back.

My dad smiles weakly. "Hey, kiddo, it looks like you're going to get to go to Los Angeles for a while. Remember Michael Sullivan?"

I stand frozen with my heart beating a zillion times a minute.

Uncle Sean puffs on his cigarette, then says, "She'd be too young. He hasn't been out here since she was almost three."

My father puts on a fake-excited smile. "He's your uncle Sean's best friend."

"Went to St. Pat's together," Uncle Sean breaks in, with the same fake smile. "He's got a girl about your age—"

I keep backing up until I feel the refrigerator handle dig in between my shoulder blades. Outrage shakes me. I'm too shocked to even cry. My stomach has no bottom, just a huge fire-breathing dragon flying up from its depths. "You're giving me away?" comes out of my mouth in someone else's voice.

"No, sweetheart, no," my dad says, looking pale and sickly

like he does when I'm being hit and he can't see me even though I'm right in front of him. "Just for part of the school year. I need some time to fix things up around here."

Part of the school year? Does he know what he's talking about? I can't go to a new school with new people! I'm starting ninth grade in one week in a place where I've already figured out how to hide. At St. Henry's, there are two buildings, the K–8 building, which has the elementary and middle school, and then the high school right next to it. Last year, at the end of the day, I slipped into the high school when all the kids were gone and I walked by the tired custodians sweeping the floors to scope out the building. I know where the lockers are and the bathrooms. I've been in the library with the scarred wooden tables and the stained-glass windows that make it feel like a church.

At St. Henry's High, I'll know how to hide so no one sees the knot of snarls in the back of my hair I can't get out or the hem falling out of my uniform. I'll know how to be invisible there.

My eyes spin around the faces of all my uncles. They all have homes. Don't any of them want me? Couldn't I stay with my cousins? "Uncle Sean, can't I stay with you?" I say.

He folds me into his big bear arms. "It's better you get

away from all this for a while, Stephanie. Your dad just needs some time to—"

I push away from him and race upstairs to my bedroom. My brush is sitting on the dresser by my bed where my mother left it, the night before last, when she was a queen and brushed my hair until it crackled. I hurl the brush against the wall. Then I slam shut my door and lock it, standing with my back pressed against it as though I could hold back the truth.

I feel my knees grow weak and sink slowly to the floor.

CHAPTER THREE

The plane is freezing and I'm wearing only shorts and a T-shirt because it was eighty and boiling in Boston when I left. I'm right in the middle of two repulsive people. On my right is a woman who has on a too-tight, shiny shirt that squeezes her stomach into loaves of fat, who keeps making little burping sounds, like she's building up for a major puke. The man on my left is skinny with glasses and major B.O.

I am one hundred percent grossed out. I look back down at *The Mystery of the Brass Bound Trunk* where Nancy is off to South America, and try to focus on the words. "*Like as not,*

Nancy will come back with her new trunk full of mysteries!" laughed Mrs. Gruen to the girl's father.

I've broken my rule about reading a Nancy Drew in public. I need it to calm my nerves. Plus, I don't care if the two rejects sitting next to me see me reading this. Between the burps and the B.O. they probably are creating too much fog to make out the title anyway.

I go back to my reading. Nancy's father just had a beautiful new trunk with Nancy's initials engraved on it show up at the Drew home in anticipation of her travel needs. My suitcase is metal and banged up. It was in our basement under an old sleeping bag that smelled like mildew.

I take out my Warrior Word notebook. I've been making this notebook since I was eleven. During lunch I go into the school library and read so I don't have to be just standing around the groups of other girls in the cafeteria like a dork with no one to talk to.

When I was younger, I had two girlfriends, Karen Fratenelli and Maggie Hogan. But then their moms found my mom drunk when they came to pick them up on Saturday morning after they slept over. Their parents wouldn't let them come over after that.

Worst of all, everyone at school found out. People started acting weird to me, saying, "Want to play hop*scotch*" or, "Stephanie, you look beery nice." Karen told me her father said, "No can do" when she asked if she could come over for even an hour after school. I don't believe she ever really even asked him. She and Maggie had already started whispering when I walked up, and then when I asked what they were talking about, they'd said, "LSPJ" (long-story-private-joke).

After that I stopped calling them. I made them into Top Enemies of Nancy Drew. I put pins in their school pictures. I tried not to think about the nights I'd spent at their houses where we brought back Martha Washington in séances, demanding that she give us a sign and screaming into each other when the candle flame flickered.

After Karen and Maggie became enemies, I just read book after book in the library at lunch and after school. Adult books by important dead people, not Nancy Drews.

When I didn't know a word, I'd put a small dot in pencil in the margin of the book and tuck a scrap of paper in between the pages so I could look it up later. On Fridays, after school, I went in and wrote down all the words in my notebook and erased the dots in the novels. On Saturdays and

Sundays, I wrote down the exact pronunciation and definition. I began thinking of these as my Warrior Words.

I've never spoken any of my Warrior Words out loud to anyone. Instead, I tend to them like baby birds, sitting on them and keeping them warm until it's time for them to hatch. Once in a while, if I'm completely alone, I'll whisper them into my hand, just to make sure they're not too frightened to actually come out of my mouth.

I stare out the plane window now, seeing my parade of words in the cottony clouds. *Clandestine*, in elongated cursive, sneaks forward followed by a hissing *surreptitious* written in wavering print. *Befuddled,* in faded block letters, stumbles across, and I feel sorry for the old professor shuffling after it, who's trying to put it back onto his shoulders.

Calmness seeps into my veins. I'm invisible when I'm watching my words. I lean back against the seat and watch *zephyr* flutter by with wispy silver letters. I'm shocked and lit with panic when the plane finally lands.

• • •

Michael Sullivan's wife, Sarah, holds up a sign that says WELCOME, STEPHANIE in giant red letters. I want to walk right by her and make my living on the streets solving cases for poor people who can't pay with money. I'd trade my skills for a hand-knit sweater or a baked ham.

Sarah looks like a mom in a TV commercial with her short brown hair, big white teeth and a honey-how-about-some-fresh-brownies smile.

I hate everything about her.

We get into her car.

"So, Stephanie," she says. "I think you should just call me Aunt Sarah."

I want to turn to her coldly and say, "Why?" Or else come up with some other rude yet funny smart-ass remark like a freckle-faced American Artful Dodger. Not that I have freckles. Or, that I'm funny.

My Catholic school training kicks in and I say, "Thanks."

I see her through my mother's contemptuous eyes. Her lack of makeup, her checkered, sexless skirt. Her daughter better not try to be friends with me. I'll grow my nails long, paint them red and scratch her eyes out. That will wipe the smile off of Aunt Sarah's face.

She takes a left turn and we are on some freeway with a million cars. "Have you ever been to Los Angeles before?" she asks in her friendly commercial mom voice.

I shake my head and then realize she can't see me since she's watching the cars. "No, I usually spend my summers abroad" pops out of my mouth.

I couldn't help it. I watch her to see what she'll say. Maybe she'll find me snippy and send me back without having to scratch the eyes out of her precious daughter.

She doesn't have time to say anything, though, because a black Mercedes cuts her off and she yells, "Jackass" in a voice that's not a mom's on a commercial at all.

I sneak another look at her. Her hands are tight on the wheel and her teeth are clenched on the right side. Maybe she's really some kind of maniac? *The Mystery of the Psychotic Driver.* I subtly check my seat belt and then sneak a hand out to grab on to the door. She cuts off the guy who cut her off, then ignores his furious honking and flipping her the bird and says, "You're going to love L.A."

CHAPTER FOUR

We are in Encino. The Sullivans live in a mansion and I know the style is Spanish from one of my mother's books on rich people's houses.

This house looks like it's right out of a Nancy Drew mystery. There are balconies with vines and two towers with little arched windows where a kidnapped princess could tap "help me" in Morse code with her feet against the wall.

Aunt Sarah pulls into a five-car garage and says, "Follow me" in a too-happy voice.

She leads me through a giant kitchen onto a patio with a

ceiling of wooden slats covered in twisting leaves. Her backyard is the size of our school football field. There are no neighbors behind it, only mountains stretching far away in jags of pine trees. I feel like I've been plunked into paradise.

A pool sparkles below jutting boulders. A waterfall spills from the mouth of a little cave. Flowers and plants I've never seen before are draped in brilliant colors all over rocks, walls and hedges.

Aunt Sarah slides into a dark green chair and motions for me to sit across from her. "Whew," she says. "This heat."

Whew what? Aunt Sarah is a wimp. Obviously she's never been to Boston in the summer. There's no humidity here. All I feel is a perfect breeze and a warm sun diluted by the lattice of vines overhead.

A woman with dark hair and eyes and wearing blue jeans comes out. I figure she's like a neighbor on a TV show who's friendly enough to come in without knocking when she says in a Spanish accent, "Mrs. Sarah, what I get you?"

"Just some lemonade and fruit for now, Carmen," Aunt Sarah says, and I narrow my eyes, thinking that maybe this woman who supposedly "works" for her was actually abducted from her happy home in a village in northern Colombia and is too afraid of the drug lords to run away.

I feel a swell of confidence in my deductive powers and picture a book cover featuring me in front of Aunt Sarah's house with a lantern in my hand, under the words *The Encino Slave Mystery.*

Carmen comes back in two seconds with a pitcher. Aunt Sarah says apologetically, "I don't know where to start, Stephanie. First, I'm sorry no one is home. Annie is at her tennis lesson, the boys are probably swimming, and Megan is still at a sleepover."

Whoa! I'm on overload. Annie, Megan, the *boys*? Dear God, let there not be brothers here. I look out at the pool shimmering in the yard. "Swimming?" I ask stupidly.

"Kills you, doesn't it?" She nods. "They barely touch it all summer. Apparently everyone swims at the tennis club down the street."

The way she says "everyone" makes me even more nervous. My plan was to find a library and hide when I wasn't in school. I hope they don't think I'm going to go swimming. I don't know how to swim. I don't even have a bathing suit.

I had pictured being housed in a garret and forced to eat disgusting food and wear rags. I figured I would suffer and later write about my experiences, but socializing and all of its horrible implications wasn't even considered.

I find my voice. "I thought you guys had only one child. One girl."

Her light green eyes open wide. "One? Oh my gracious. Michael Junior's the oldest; he's twenty and home for the summer from Stanford. Then there's Patrick and Danny, the twins, fraternal, not identical, they're nineteen and home from Berkeley. Then Annie, she was fourteen in March, she's—a couple years older than you?"

My cheeks burn. "I was fourteen last February."

She laughs totally unaware of my humiliation and makes it worse. "You're such a little thing I just thought—"

She's distracted by a loud noise in the kitchen like a chair turning over. I hear low voices and loud laughter and what sounds like shoving. Dread stuns me. Older boys.

I want a quick earthquake to crash the house so I'm spared meeting them. I never talk to older boys. I even keep my distance from those who are my cousins, staying out of their way as they go by in a herd of sweatshirts, footballs, big feet and grunts.

"Boys," Aunt Sarah calls out gaily. "Come out here, there's someone I want you to meet."

More noise. It sounds like fighting. Three blond heads of

hair flashing over tanned faces and torsos come spilling out of the sliding patio doors. I'm mortified to be sitting here with a piece of fruit in my mouth as if I just sit and eat fruit all day long.

"This is Stephanie. She's going to be staying with us for a while."

"Hey," one of them calls out and they start to troop back into the house.

I feel a spark of relief at their departure, which Aunt Sarah ruins by snapping, "Gentlemen."

They stop.

"Now, how about some introductions," she says.

I'm double-dying now as they all walk right up to me. The tallest one sticks out his hand and says, "Enchanted to meet you. I'm Michael."

I hate Aunt Sarah for doing this to me. I look at his face and he's really, really cute with green eyes and wavy hair. I don't know if he's kidding with the "enchanted" or if he's saying that because he's rich and that's how rich people talk. I'm so embarrassed I'm almost choking. I put my hand in his and focus on doing a solid shake. "Stephanie O'Hagen," I say solemnly.

He gives me a slightly surprised look, and then one of his brothers knocks him across the back of the head and says to me, “I’m the smart twin, Daniel. The dunce next to me is Patrick.”

I realize that Daniel is almost as cute as Michael but with a skinnier nose and a slightly longer chin. Patrick looks like both of his brothers but is somehow not really cute at all, so I’m the least afraid of him. I figure he stares in the mirror while he’s shaving with a sad face, thinking he got the short end of the genetic stick.

“All right, you can go back to being savages,” Aunt Sarah says.

They fall back into the kitchen, leaving me breathless. Then, a little girl of about seven comes out onto the patio and cries, “Mommy!” as she falls into Aunt Sarah’s arms.

For a second, I’m ignored as Aunt Sarah pulls her on her lap and asks her questions about some sleepover. After some hugging, tickling and kissing she introduces her to me as “Megan.” I swallow the metallic taste of jealousy in my mouth before I can fake a nice “Hi.”

• • •

I'm unpacking in a beautiful apricot bedroom when there's a quick knock followed by the door flying open. I'm so happy it's not one of the older boys that it takes me a minute to absorb the girl who walks in and sits on the edge of the bed.

"Hi," she says before I say a word. "I'm Annie. I'm so sorry I wasn't in when you got here. Tennis. I want to hear everything about Boston."

She speaks in a rush of enthusiasm and makes me almost as nervous as her brothers do. She's the perfect daughter to the commercial mom. About a head taller than I am, she is blond with big blue eyes, long tanned limbs and perky, bra-sheltered breasts.

My first thought is one of utter relief that I don't have to share a bedroom with her so that she won't see my barely raised nipples in my training bra. I have no doubt she's been having her period for years.

"Hi." I manage a smile. "I'm Stephanie."

"And, you're from Boston." She flips her long tresses out of her eyes. "Okay, say, 'Park the car.' "

I speak normally. "Paak the caa."

She squeals. "God, I love that! Do it again."

We spend the next ten minutes with me doing words on

command. I don't care that I'm the trained monkey. I feel a sudden violent urge of wanting her to like me. That I want to be part of her life even if it's only as a moon to her shining, golden sun.

• • •

Annie whispers to me on the way down to dinner. "Just be glad today's not Carmen's day off. My mom is, like, the worst cook in the world. You'd probably turn around and fly home."

I feel a tug in my stomach, a glimmer of the familiar ache. I see our tiny house with the ungroomed lawn, the dark green couch with stains from the time she threw up. Curtains kept shut all day because the light gives her a headache. The scarred Formica table. Burnt popcorn I've made myself, sprinkled with parmesan cheese because I read that cheese is protein and protein makes you grow. A book in front of me so that I'm anywhere but there. "My mom's not a great cook either," I say in the same tone she uses, thinking as I say it, This is how girls talk.

We walk into their enormous kitchen. The boys are already sitting down. Michael looks at me as we walk in and I have to turn away. On the table, chicken steams from a platter next to bowls of corn, noodles and salad. Carmen is running back and forth with rolls and salt and pepper shakers. Aunt Sarah is asking who wants iced tea.

Annie nudges me and says, "Welcome to the madhouse. My mom said you're an only child. You're probably not used to this kind of craziness."

I slide thankfully into a chair next to Annie. I feel less exposed than when I was standing up. What if Michael noticed my training bra?

There's an empty seat at the head of the table. Annie notices my glance. "Dad's probably with a client."

Client? Did she say "client"? Delight surges forward like a baseball someone just slugged into the outfield. "A client, then he's a lawy— "

I don't get to finish my question. A tall man in a dark blue suit with hair graying slightly at the temples walks in and looks straight at me. "Welcome, Sean O'Hagen's niece."

I know I'm supposed to say, "Thank you, it's good to be here," but I'm starstruck. I'm looking straight into the face of Carson Drew.

I'm torn between wanting everyone to get up and leave so that I can sit alone and question him, and having them stay and keep him talking, just so I can stare at him. I finally smile and say, "Hi, Mr. Sullivan."

He says, "Call me Uncle Michael," then kisses his wife and says, "Queen Anne" with a little bow to Annie, who rolls her eyes at me. He walks down the table and tickles Megan under the chin before kissing her and saying, "Princess Megan."

He makes his way all the way around the table, gently cuffing his sons on the head as he goes. When he gets to me, he kisses me on the top of my head and I feel pleasure zinging from my hair follicles into my toes. I glance across at Annie, who's rolling her eyes again, so I immediately hide my happiness.

While Uncle Michael settles into his seat and puts his napkin on his lap, Annie leans across the table and whispers to me, "My dad is such a spaz."

I feel a lightning flash of rage at her and I pray he didn't hear her say that and think on any level that I invited it. He seems fine as he says, "So tell me, how is your uncle Sean?"

I say, "Fine," then watch spellbound as he goes around the table asking about everyone's day and then telling a funny story about court. Annie doesn't even know, as we get up from the table to go upstairs, that I've decided to steal her father.

CHAPTER FIVE

Lights sparkle from houses on either side of the dark road. I listen to the excited rise and fall of Annie's voice as we walk down the hilly streets of her neighborhood. I study everything she does. The thought of walking with a friend is as heady as a dream. I nod when she nods. I laugh when she laughs. I think, *I'm doing it, I'm doing it.*

She walks fast but not too fast. Her hips swing out. A mom from one of the houses calls for her son, Ronnie, and Annie giggles wildly so I join in and wonder who or what we're laughing at. She speaks almost nonstop, filling me in on "the gang," her cluster of girlfriends whom she sees at the club every day and speaks to, texts or IM's until almost midnight every night.

I force myself not to express surprise at her wealth of friends, comforts and freedoms. I nod when she pauses at various points, to suggest that I, too, live in a world of endless gossip and Internet fashion consultations.

While she speaks, I feel a wide flicker of emptiness ride up my legs and settle in my stomach. Hazy images of desires I've felt all my life come into sharp focus. I want her friends, her pool, her breasts and her parents. I want to be so secure in knowing my father cares about me that I could roll my eyes when he says something and warn a friend that he's a spaz.

As we climb up the hill, I look down at the glittering lights in the valley below. The wind brings more new fragrances that twirl up my nose and burst into wildly colored flowers in my brain. I watch Annie out of the corner of my eye as she speaks, trying to memorize how she opens her eyes bigger to emphasize a point and how she flips her hair over her shoulder with an impatient flick of her wrist at the end of a statement.

We stop at the end of Annie's street, which, she tells me, turns into "Mulholland." I roll the word around my tongue and see it in my head in big strong letters followed by hard-muscled twenty-year-old boys in bathing suits with dark tans and flashing green eyes.

We walk down Mulholland. The houses stop and dirt and woods rise to our right. Annie grabs my elbow and jerks her head toward the woods. A light flickers ahead of us, off to the right. Annie does a lousy imitation of an owl. Another lousy owl hoots back. Annie giggles and says, "Leslie is hilarious."

We start down the dirt path splashed with pebbles. Annie pulls out a tiny flashlight from her pocket and snaps it on, letting the thin ray of light bounce over her pink-painted toes in supple brown sandals.

I'm ashamed of my blue tennis shoes that are slightly curled at the toes because I had to put them in the dryer after I got caught in the rain. I hope she doesn't shine the light on them. I point ahead to distract her. "That way?" I ask.

"Righto, Watson," she says and I wonder if she meant to say, "Righto, Livingston."

She walks quickly and I follow, although it's hard because I can't see any of the light from the flashlight on the ground in front of me. I can only follow the dim shadows of her legs.

The wind is strong. A bug flies into my eye. I blink furiously, following Annie's legs up to her blue jean shorts and gleaming white T-shirt. I suddenly hate the shorts and shirt I have on and find it unbearable to be seen in them when I meet her gang. With new clarity I see my outfit as something her little sister, Megan, would wear, red shorts with a matching red-and-white-striped shirt, except it's so faded that the white stripes look gray. It was a hand-me-down from one of my older cousins. Even though my mom always had fancy new clothes, there was no point in wasting money on me. I once heard her tell my aunt Clare that she could dress me in boys' clothes for all the difference it would make.

We're twisting and turning up the path when there's a rustling in the bushes ahead of us. Annie turns around and whispers, "Coyotes."

I'm shocked but excited. I anticipate a circle around us with cruel fangs and yellow eyes. Annie picks up a branch and lunges low at the bush. Scurrying feet scratch. I look around for another branch to defend myself and she says, "They're gone. Total wimps."

She laughs a throaty woman's laugh, and I see her perfect teeth shimmer against the soft outline of her tan face. Without seeing her eyes clearly I know they widen when she says, "Let's tell everyone we're real cousins."

For a moment I'm stunned by her generosity, and then the moon flickers and I see my short shadow next to her tall one and realize the fun she'll have at her friends' outbursts of disbelief because of our contrast. The "no ways!" because of her aura of gold and my immigrant-looking darkness. There's another owl hoot and Annie suddenly turns off the path and presses through a lattice of branches, one of which slaps back at me, landing a stinging blow on my cheek.

"Ow," I cry out, tears springing into my eyes.

She turns quickly to me. "Omigod, did that get you?" She shines the flashlight on my cheek. "I'm such an idiot," she says, running her finger over what I imagine to be a ferocious welt.

Under her examination, my hostility fades. She's very attentive with her mouth pressed into a line of concentration. She takes her finger from my face, grabs me around the shoulder in a hard hug and says, "Sorry, cuz, can you ever forgive me?"

I'm embarrassed but delighted to be the source of so much concern. I'm thinking of the perfect graceful word to let her know I'm okay when she grabs me by both shoulders, gets two inches from my face and yells, "Maaaaaw," making her mouth into a long O shape.

I don't even know how to compute this when three other "Maaaaaw"s spring up beside us. I see her grab other shoulders of shadowy figures and one at a time say "Maaaaaw" back to them. Then she puts her arm around my shoulder and says, "Ladies, this is my cousin Stephanie." She pauses, does the big eyes and adds, "She's from Boston." She ends on a hair flip.

The figures crowd closer. Flashlight beams hit me. People talk at once. Somebody says, "I love Boston. My cousin goes to Harvard." Someone else asks if I know someone named Cathy Gerby, who's from Vermont.

Before I can answer anyone, Annie says, "Girls, girls, girls, let's sit down and be civilized" in a voice that I think must be one of their teachers because they all laugh. Everyone sits down in the spot where they're standing and throws their flashlights into the middle so it's a flashlight bonfire.

Annie points to a girl with auburn hair and big blue eyes. "This is Leslie."

I make eye contact with Leslie, the one who's supposed to be hilarious. Leslie bows her head and says, "Pleased to meet you, ma'am" in a guy's southern accent and the other girls laugh, so I do too.

I note with enormous relief that Leslie doesn't seem to be that much taller than I am. She is, however, well into puberty. Big round breasts jut from beneath her green tank top. I sigh, and then notice she's plump with fleshy arms and thick thighs. It occurs to me, as I process the totality of her physique, that maybe I could eat my way into boobs, just making sure that I stop after I get them so I don't gain extra weight anywhere else.

I feel such a warmth toward Leslie for this revelation that I say, "Pleased to meet you too" in her same southern gentleman voice. I get the same laughs Leslie did, and I'm heady with the flicker of pride that flashes across Annie's face, like, "Hey, my cousin's cool."

I want to hold on to the moment of my first spontaneous social remark, but it's already forgotten as Annie tosses a pebble at the legs of the girl sitting across from her and says, " . . . and in this corner, our math and science genius of the year, Eva Bennett."

Eva purses her lips and stares at me fiercely while she says to Annie in a friendly voice, "Enough about that stupid award."

Something about her chills the warmth blazing through

me from my Leslie triumph. Her eyes are almost as black as mine but small and tight, glittery as a snake's. Her nose is sharp, her cheekbones slashing. Her hair is pulled back into a large black ponytail, and she's pale and fashion model thin. I can tell she's very tall by the long legs she has crossed in a casual Indian style.

I say, "Hi, Eva."

She nods and says, "My uncle's a physician in Boston. He lives on Beacon Street. Dr. Dennis Bennett? Maybe you know him? Where in Boston do you live?"

Her eyes bore into me as if she can see my mother passed out on the couch and the pile of laundry that heaves over the hamper like vomit.

Supercilious in wiry letters spikes up into my brain and then turns into a red arrow and stabs me with hate. I feel nauseated from the threat of exposure when I give the address that will tell her that I am everything she is not.

Annie flips her hair and I'm filled with a flash of genius. I adopt Annie's excited wide eyes. "Omigod," I say. "My aunt Rose went to your uncle! I remember hearing that name. She said he was fantastic. She loved him!"

"Ahnt, ahnt, ahnt," Leslie imitates me, then looks at Annie. "I love the way she talks."

I look guilelessly past Eva and latch onto the last girl. "And the best for last?"

This earns me a big smile from a girl who is like a sleepy peach. She should be pretty with her light brown hair, green eyes and perfect skin, but she isn't. Maybe her older sister is a knockout or her mom was at her age.

"Hi, I'm Emily," she says and looks almost embarrassed to be the center of attention, even for a second. Her shoulders slope so at first I think she's humiliated by her lack of development like I am. Then she swats a mosquito and I see two perfectly acceptable breasts jiggle.

Annie claps her hands together. "Here, here, here. Having made all the introductions with my eastern seaboard cousin, who's got the goods?"

The goods? Like goodies?

I try to keep the wrinkles out of my forehead and look just as casual as the other girls while Eva fumbles in her backpack. If it's cookies, I hope they're chocolate.

Eva pulls out a silver case, and for a moment I see my mother's red flashing nails and silver bangles pulling out a long Virginia Slim.

Eva pulls out a shorter cigarette. "Marlboro Light?" she says, tipping the case toward me.

"Ah, sure," I say. "Thanks." I reach out and take a cigarette, for the first time in my life touching one that isn't smashed in the bottom of an ashtray that I'm cleaning.

"Brand okay?" Eva says, keeping an eye on me as she tosses another cigarette to Leslie.

My "Um, fine" is muffled by Annie's scratching through Eva's backpack for a lighter. Eva sits back, pleased with the obvious display of Annie's comfort and familiarity with her possessions.

While Annie rummages, Eva focuses back on me. I feel her eyes like two scalpels on me, eager to cut back my fragile layers and show everyone how dirty I am inside. "Cute outfit," she says. Her tone is neutral on the surface, but her eyes are scornful and mocking. I can tell she's disappointed when none of the other girls turn to stare at my pathetic red-and-gray-striped shirt.

"Finally," Annie says, pulling out Eva's lighter. She expertly flicks the lighter, holding it to the end of her cigarette until it glows like a dark red firefly. She tosses Eva the lighter. Eva sticks her cigarette in the side of her mouth and ignites her lighter, but instead of lighting her own cigarette first, she holds the lighter up to me. Her nails are short and manicured with a dark brown polish.

For a moment, I watch the tiny flame arch against the black night. It reminds me of the candles at church and guilt flickers in my stomach. I've got two seconds to decide if this is a sin and if so, of what magnitude.

I know it's not one of the commandments and I know it's not listed anywhere I've read. I tuck my cigarette in the corner of my mouth and lean close to the flame Eva holds in front of my face, breathing in the way I watched Annie do it. Smoke curls into my throat. I desperately need to cough, but I can tell that Eva is praying I will.

I hold the smoke in as it scorches the pale pink lining of my windpipe. I picture the roof of my mouth blackened with ripples of cancer breaking the surface in little white pustules. Tears spring to my eyes that I hope are swallowed by the darkness. I'll die before I let myself cough. I stare at Eva and slowly let the smoke out through the small O of my mouth. As if bored, she turns away from me.

We smoke quietly for a while as if we've all put in a long day in construction and it's time for a well-deserved break. Annie leans her head back and exhales gray puffs that thin out as they climb to the trees. Our flashlight campfire glows. The wind ruffles my hair and the moon is almost full with streaks of clouds over it. It is a perfect setting to bring back

Martha Washington in a séance, but I don't suggest it because I'm sure it's too babyish.

Eva lights a new cigarette off of her old one and leans forward. "Who's up for T or D?"

"Yesss!" Annie cries. "Leslie's first."

"Why do I have to go first?"

"Because you went to the bridge with Ben last night."

"Really?" Emily heaves. "Oh, she's definitely first."

Leslie hides her face behind her hands, but by the way she's laughing, I know she's excited to go first.

"Truth or dare," Annie barks.

Leslie says, "Truth" immediately. Apparently giving the choice is just a formality. The girls all bend in toward Leslie, ready to devour her words.

"How far did you go with Ben last night?" Annie asks.

Leslie groans as though this was the one question she'd hoped they wouldn't ask.

I realize that I'm nervous about what I'm about to hear, afraid I won't be able to offer reciprocal experiences of my own.

"Well," Leslie says, running her hand through her hair. "I let him . . ." She buries her head, then wiggles her first and middle finger.

The other girls scream. My stomach tightens. Even though I've been stuck in Catholic school, I've known about the time-honored sign for showing that a guy put his hand in your pants since sixth grade. I've just never known anyone who personally participated.

I look at Leslie to see if I would have guessed, just by looking at her, that this is a girl who did this.

I force an expression of casual interest on my face and then notice in alarm that my cigarette ash has become abnormally long. I tap it off violently, and then hope no one notices as I stub it out clumsily in the dirt.

I pray I'm not up next.

"How about our little Bostonian," Eva yells, fake-friendly. "T or D?"

The other girls shift to get a better look at me. Leslie looks slightly miffed that more inquiry wasn't made into her bold venture into womanhood.

I'm dying. "Truth," I say, as I know there's only one choice.

I can taste the bitter nicotine on my tongue and the insides of my cheeks. I wonder if there's a slight scum of smoke on my teeth.

"How far have you gone?" Eva demands.

I look quickly at Annie as if she might say, "Hey, guys, this is between my cousin and me," but she's leaning forward, an eager wolf like the rest of them.

I'm desperate to come up with the correct answer. I have no idea if Leslie is the norm or the deviation. Is she the first of them to do it or the last? Is it worse to appear inexperienced or a slut? Not that they seem to consider Leslie a slut, but maybe her allowing a guy to put his hand in her pants is excused precisely because of the magnitude of her bosom, as if its primitive cry could not be denied.

I feel a slight sweat on my upper lip and want to wipe it, but I don't want to let them see me wiping it. At the last second I blurt, "Just feeling up," because I fear Eva may ask me specifics about the experience of fingering.

Eva rakes her eyes over my minuscule breasts, then says, laughing, "That must have been quick." Everyone laughs, even Annie, and I hate them all so much I want to raise a stick and puncture the very breasts that give them the arrogance to laugh at mine.

Instead, I force a half smile on my face, its frozen curve growing hard as I wait for the laughter to ebb and it to be someone else's turn.

CHAPTER SIX

The whole Sullivan family now knows I don't have a bathing suit. Annie came bounding into my room this morning and said we were going to the club today. I told her that I "forgot" my bathing suit and she immediately screamed, "Omigod! She comes to L.A. with no bathing suit. Omigod!"

Her brothers were just stumbling out of their rooms to go to breakfast and she did a "Maaaaaw" right in one of their faces and repeated the whole thing even louder.

Hearing this, Aunt Sarah began scrambling in their attic and has come into my room with one of Annie's old suits she'd been meaning to donate. They both stand there as if they are expecting me to strip and try it on right in front of them.

I force myself to act excited and thank her for the suit. I tell her I'm sure it will be perfect and that I'll just put it on at the club.

I'm really thinking that maybe I'll get hit by a car on the way and never have to do it. I have no intention of meeting any more of Annie's terrifying friends with their aggressive puberty and vast sexual experience. After my turn last night, Annie disclosed that she had let her tennis instructor, John Keswick III, do the finger thing.

We never got to Eva's sexual history. After the "omigods" and "no ways" about Annie and a discussion about when (a week ago), where (his parents' house) and if they would hook up again (yes!), Eva looked at her watch and said she had to get home by nine thirty because her parents were coming in from Europe.

Today, everyone's meeting at their club at ten. Annie tells me she can't wait for me to meet "the guys" and John Keswick III. John is seventeen and Annie says everyone mostly calls him JKIII because he's one of those "the thirds." He's not a real tennis instructor. He just helps out in the summer because he's like number one on the school tennis team and the club pro loves him. Annie said her parents would kill her if they found out she was going out with him.

I wish I didn't have to meet him. I've never spoken to a seventeen-year-old boy in my life, much less one who has put his hands all over my sort-of cousin. What if he asks me questions about Boston like Eva did? What if he knows that I know what he did? Even worse, what if he sees me in a bathing suit and says, "Hey, is your cousin, like, twelve?"

I could totally die.

I wish I required immediate hospitalization for something. I stopped thinking God was good when my mom threw me down the stairs and gave me a concussion when I was ten. He could really make a comeback now if he'd just strike me ill. Nothing major, just like appendicitis or tonsillitis, so the doctor, who would have white hair and a TV-dad face, could tell Aunt Sarah, "I'm sorry, but this young lady isn't going to be doing any swimming for a long, long time."

I'm considering saying I'm sick when Annie says, "Let's go!" and races downstairs into the kitchen. I follow her because I don't know what else to do. She grabs two glasses and pours us orange juice. I'm hoping maybe Aunt Sarah will come down and we'll have a long, leisurely breakfast, but Annie downs her juice in about thirty seconds and says, "Let's start diets and not eat anything else today."

Despite the rumble of hunger in my stomach and my commitment to eating my way into boobs, there's no way I'm going to ask for anything, even though I saw her brothers eating Pop-Tarts, which we never had at home because my mom always said they were too expensive.

We go into Annie's garage and she hops on a beautiful blue bike, motioning to an equally perfect red one beside it. "You can ride my old one," she says.

We pedal off down her street and I don't ask why she needed a new bike, as I am for the moment thrilled with the smooth glide of the wheels and the brilliant flowers that flicker by us like jumbled jewels. It doesn't even matter that I can't sit on the seat while my feet are on the pedals.

After twenty minutes we pull up the wide driveway of the Bennington Country Club. It looks like a judge's mansion because it has big white pillars and black shutters. We park our bikes at the bike rack and lock them while Annie says, "I can't wait 'til I get my license. A couple years from now I'll be cruising up here in a convertible."

We carry our backpacks to the side gate where the pool is and Annie signs us in. The pool is enormous and shimmering. Half the lanes are blocked off with lines of black buoys for serious swimmers. A huge sundeck is to our left. Beneath it is a snack bar with little tables and a counter with stools. To our right is the ladies' locker room. My backpack is heavy against my shoulder. Inside it is a rolled-up towel and in the middle of the towel is the bathing suit, huddled like a sleeping snake.

Annie hurries into the locker room. I follow her, my feet heavy as if my tennis shoes were made of wet concrete. She tosses her backpack onto a wooden bench. "You can use my locker for your stuff," she says. She pulls off her shirt and I feel a strange panic at the sight of her womanly breasts inside a white bra.

I scoot toward the stall ahead of us and say over my shoulder, "I just have to pee."

Inside the stall I feel so much pressure I could burst. I open my backpack and take out the towel. I hadn't really even looked at the bathing suit at the house. I just rolled it up in the towel as if it would bite me if I held it too long. I pull out the top with a shaking hand. It's a blue band with black flowers. A whisper of relief caresses me—at least there are no cups, which would lie empty until a wayward arm or leg in the pool knocked into one of them and crushed it.

I pull off my shirt and my training bra. I hook the bathing suit top in the front and slide it around to the back. Next, I step out of my shorts and underwear and put on the bottoms. Annie shouts, "Hurry up" through the door. I stuff my shorts and top into the backpack, and then open the door and hurry to the locker, afraid to make eye contact with Annie, who stands like a beach beauty right out of *The O.C.* in her orange-and-green bikini.

"Let's go," she says, grabbing my arm, and as we rush into the sun, I catch a glimpse of us in the mirror, a tall blur of tan, blond, orange and green, followed by a short blend of olive, black, blue and purple.

I blink in the sunlight. "They're up on the sundeck," she says, and I follow her smooth back with the indented waist up redwood stairs. Music blasts from someone's iPod dock as we reach the top. Warm coconut oil mingles with the scent of some woman's coffee and cigarette. Ahead of me, at the far end of the sundeck, is a wall of guys.

Panic beats like a bird trapped in my chest. We walk closer. Annie tosses her head and her hair flashes like gold. We're so close now I can hear the low hum of the guys' voices and I think I can smell their guy sweat.

I really need to get out of here, but there is absolutely no escape. Annie is jittery—I feel an invisible substance that jumps from the guys to her and back again. Half-naked bodies are pressing all around me. I can't breathe. I feel small but on display, something so grossly inadequate that everyone will be compelled to look only to drop their eyes, shiver, and wish they hadn't looked in the first place.

My breath stops. Black rises in front of me. I'm about to faint, but at the last second I crawl up inside my head and beg for my words to save me. *Stentorian* storms through my brain as blasts of male laughter hit my ears. I can breathe again. I can even let the words disappear and look around me at the girls lying on their beach towels.

Waves of calm take the tightness out of my chest. I'm a witness, not a participant. I'm Nancy Drew getting information for the case she's trying to solve. None of these people are people I have to know. Just a collection of faces and names whose words will become part of my report to my father, Carson Drew.

I look over at the wall of guys without fear and my eyes land on a strip of tight tanned stomach over a pair of blue bathing trunks. For a second, blood beats into my face, and then I remember I'm safe from this hot flesh with my Warrior Words, marching in my mind, while I just observe. When *lascivious* and *turgid* pounce into my thoughts, I even smile slightly, thinking of the books with bosoms on them I found under my mother's side of the bed, and all the words I learned from them.

"That's John Keswick III," Annie whispers, following my gaze and I look up from the blue bathing trunks to a muscular torso and the face of a movie star. He smiles, flashing perfect white teeth. He's very tan with thick sandy brown hair, a man's jaw and bright blue eyes.

"Hey," he says, dropping the hand with his iPhone as we walk closer, but he's not looking at both of us. He only sees Annie.

I peek at her, a stolen sideways glance. She grows in luster beside me. Beams of light glint from her hair. A fuzzy force field of hormones whirls around her body. Words from a National Geographic documentary we watched in social studies pop into my head: *When the Yanamamo female is ready for marriage, she is dressed in rich tribal colors and brought to a neighboring clan for inspection.*

"Am I getting a lesson today?" she asks JKIII. "I think I forgot my racket."

Giggling rises from the towels spread on the deck, and I look down and focus on the girls spread out in front of me. Leslie and Emily are slathered in suntan oil and hunched over a Facebook message on Leslie's BlackBerry. Eva has a hat on and probably lots of sunscreen because of her fair skin. She's not even aware of the other two girls, but in her own world, texting on her iPhone.

That's something that you don't see in my neighborhood in Boston. Even though most kids have cell phones by the end of eighth grade, no one has a BlackBerry or an iPhone because they're way too expensive. Most kids have one or two old Dell computers at home and have to wait for other sibs to do term papers and homework before they can check their Facebooks.

I, of course, don't have any kind of phone since when I suggested to my mom that we both get one, she said that if God had wanted her to be a prisoner of technology, she would have been born with a metal chip in her head.

I never even brought up getting Facebook, even though we have a computer on the desk in the living room that my dad uses for law school, because the whole point of that is having friends to keep up with.

Leslie says to me, "Throw your towel down here," and slides hers over to make room.

The direct contact wrenches me completely out of my safe observation surrounded by Warrior Words. I'm back, underdeveloped and exposed, on a sundeck in Los Angeles with kids who send sexual signals to each other so strong I can almost smell them. Hurriedly, I unroll my towel next to hers and lie down on my stomach so no one will notice my chest.

Leslie sits up holding a bottle of suntan lotion. "Do you want me to do your back?" she asks. "Emily already did mine."

I nod, caught off guard in this world of reciprocal female acts. She rubs the cream over my back. Her hands are strong and warm. The sun feels good. "You should undo your strap," she tells me. "You'll get a mark."

The minute attention paid to a detail of having a tan line across my back pleases me to no end. I feel a wild surge of gratitude for Leslie that she should take such an interest in me.

I bunch up my towel under my chest and unhook my

strap. Leslie rubs cream in the spot that has become socially precious. I close my eyes for a second, enjoying the warmth of the sun and smells from lotion, flowers, and the cinnamon Orbit that Leslie cracks.

The mood is broken by Leslie's friendly voice. "Guys," she says. "Have you met Annie's cousin Stephanie?"

The wall of teenage boys moves, differentiates. I think of bees clustered into a humming mosaic until they finally fly away, yielding views of the individuals. I can tell there are four of them. JKIII is on the far right standing next to Annie, who flips her hair and says, "Omigod, I'm, like, so rude. Guys, this is Stephanie."

All the eyes turn to me. I'm stuck in a quarter-seal, arching up partially from my stomach with my chest covered up by the towel and my back naked. I'm still warmed by Leslie's touch and her concern about a potential pale streak across my back, so I'm emboldened enough to be social. "Hi," I call out as if I'm Nancy Drew sandwiched by her girlfriends, Bess and George, when their collegiate-sweatered boyfriends, Ned, Burt and Dave arrive.

"You have to hear the way she talks," Annie says. "Stephanie, say—"

"Annie's old suit," Eva interrupts, walking around me as if

I'm one of those frogs we dissected in science class who's lying on a little board with its legs and arms pinned down. "I was trying and trying to think of where I'd seen your bathing suit before, then suddenly it came to me. It was Annie's, like, two years ago."

Red rushes my face. Eva's raised eyebrows and satisfied smirk scorch holes in my brain. Desert air rises from my throat and my tongue sticks to the roof of my mouth.

JKIII snaps an irritated glance at Eva, then looks back to Annie and says, "Annie, what did you want Stephanie to say?"

A couple of the other guys look at Annie also, waiting to be entertained. I'm stunned with the realization that the guy mind hasn't even grasped the enormity of my humiliation. That none of them seem to get the direct correlation between wearing a bathing suit someone wore at twelve and being physically immature. I'm giddy with the idea that the guys here just think Eva was interrupting with some boring talk about clothes.

Annie flips hair over one shoulder. "Okay, her best stuff is with r's. Like, ask her to say, 'How far is that car?'"

Everyone's eyes are on me as JKIII says, "Say, 'How far is that car?'"

I half roll my eyes to Leslie, who giggles, and then I say, "How faa is that caa?"

Annie squeals, "Don't you love that?"

A guy standing next to JKIII says, "Say 'idea.'"

I give a little shrug. "Idear."

He nods vigorously. "I knew it. We went to the Cape two summers ago. They all do that." He smiles at me and seems pleased, as if I've done him proud.

JKIII fist-bumps the guy and says, "Little bro, remembering the Cape."

The boy, I guess his brother, takes a little bow and Annie jerks her head at him. "This is Brian."

I give a self-conscious nod. He's really cute. Not as cute as JKIII, but he has the same bright blue eyes and big smile. He's just a little shorter and not quite as muscular, and his hair is darker. I figure he's probably around two years younger than his brother, more like fifteen.

"And this is Andrew." She flips her hand toward a tall boy with black curly hair, fierce brown eyes, and his arm in a cast. He doesn't smile, but looks at me hard as if to see if I'm something at which he should also be angry.

"Hi," I say.

"Hey," he returns. He doesn't turn away. He keeps staring

at me. I can't stop staring at him. He's got something in the back of his eyes, something so raging I'd expect to see him in my neighborhood in Boston. He doesn't seem to belong on this porch of privilege where everyone only needs to care about tans or tennis games. He suddenly snaps his eyes away from me like it's okay for him to try to find out what I'm hiding, but not for me to see into him.

"And this is Matt," Annie's social director voice cuts in. The boy next to Andrew is shorter, with straight brown hair and green eyes. "Bri, Andrew and Matt are all the same grade as us."

I nod again, vaguely relieved that at least all the guys that I'll have to see are not older and, thus, exponentially terrifying.

I start to settle back onto my towel to try to relax when I feel Eva's eyes boring into me again. She's nothing if not relentless, and I can tell she's furious that her observation of me wearing Annie's old suit didn't unleash an outpouring of derision over my obviously immature body, or, at least, a torrent of covert, smug looks between all the girls.

She's studying me hard. Her math and science brain is analyzing facts. There is something bothering her. Something about me that's not adding up. I don't belong in this world. She can feel the false premise throwing off her calculations, and she won't rest until she unmasks me. She's seen the old and unfashionable outfit I wore last night. Now she's observed that I don't have a bathing suit of my own.

Suddenly, a light pierces her eyes, like she's discovered the cure for cancer. Dread spreads through my stomach and I prepare for her next assault.

"Hey, Stephanie," she purrs, walking up to me. "Why don't you show us some pictures of your peeps in Boston. Then maybe you can tell them about us and we can all become friends."

Becoming "friends" means only one thing. She's demanding to see my Facebook and she's, of course, noticed that I haven't once texted or BBM'ed in her presence while the others have done it endlessly in the same time frame.

In an instant, I know, she is hoping to reveal that I don't have a cool phone or BlackBerry. If I do whip out a phone and pull up my Facebook, she's hoping I won't have that many friends and that those I have will be obvious losers. I'm sure she can't even imagine that I'm not on Facebook. That would be a jackpot for her of unbelievable proportion.

Her idea sparks immediate interest from everyone. I know from overhearing kids at school that everyone is always trying to expand their number of Facebook friends. That it is the ultimate validation of one's worth as a person to have hundreds of people wanting to read about their every mood and activity. The girls all look eager to check out their eastern competition, and even the boys seem curious to scope out the female inhabitants of my exotically accented city and maybe have a few cyber hookups.

"Great idea," Annie screams. "We can be friends with some of your friends and then finally meet them in college!"

Someone says that Annie is a "friend ho" and that she'll do anything to increase her number, which is already up to 438. I don't even register who said it because I'm quaking with terror. Within seconds, I'm going to be exposed as electronically naked and without the rich social network that they so easily take for granted.

I have to think fast. The girls and guys are looking at me with deep excitement and Eva has a cruel smile curving her lips as if she's already pictured me disgraced.

I mentally scramble for a strategy. Something. Anything. I have no idea how to navigate out of this. No *Mystery of the Fraudulent Facebooker* to guide me.

Suddenly, I picture this girl from St. Henry's High, Maria Giarelli, an eleventh grader who was actually suspended for the last month of school. The high school scandal, of course, leaked into our school and even I heard about it, just by standing around the other kids. Would it really be so bad if I just borrowed a little something from her life?

"Um," I drop my voice. "Do I really have to go into this in front of the guys?"

This, of course, makes the guys lean in even closer. I sigh heavily, just like Leslie did when she was about to disclose how far she went with Ben in Truth or Dare last night. "I, ah, got shut down."

"What does that mean?" Eva demands.

"My Facebook got shut down and my phone confiscated for two months."

There's a collective intake of breath. I scan the eager faces, which are awaiting the titillating details. Everyone knows there's pretty much only one reason this ever happens and it always has something to do with sex.

"So, there was this high school party," I begin.

Smiles crack. Stories about high school parties always promise good stuff about bad behavior. "Some people got sort of wild. And, I, ah, posted the 'inappropriate photographs.'" I make my voice sound like a really uptight teacher, thinking that's how Annie would do it.

"Ni-ice," JKIII says, and the guys join in with appreciative laughter. Annie looks at me like I'm some kind of brilliant, gutsy rebel and Andrew stares in complete fascination.

Eva boils.

"Anyway, some loser, who I never should have confirmed on my Facebook, snitched me off to the nuns at my school, who freaked out. And that's when they confiscated my phone," I say.

A few mutters rise over the treachery of the loser snitch. Then Leslie sits up, breaks out a bag of Doritos from her backpack and holds them out to the boys. Andrew says, "Cheese?" and when she says, "But of course," in kind of a French accent, he sits down next to her on her towel. I don't look at him, but I can feel him about two inches from my rib cage.

A nervous humming spreads through my body, silent yet expedient, as if my blood is rushing to warn all my nerve endings. I shut my eyes in case anyone peeks in and sees my fear. I can hear Andrew munching on the Doritos when something lands on the center of my back. I force my face into a casual "what's up" look, then open my eyes and glance over at him. He's chewing with his mouth open.

There are orange crumbs in the corner of his lips, but I'm focused only on his eyes.

"Let's just leave it there," he says, referring to what I guess is the Dorito he tossed onto my back. "Then, by the end of the day, we'll take it off and you'll have the perfect shape of a chip."

He confuses me utterly. His words are joking, but in the back of his eyes I see a thin curtain covering muscular, shadowy dancers who move in perfect rhythm together, yet clearly hate each other.

I don't know what to do about the chip on my back. I have a sense Annie would rise up in fake fury and say, "You're getting it now" and maybe throw something at him and then run screaming from him when he chased her.

I don't think I could pull this off. I'd have to have a fun tone of voice, and I've never had one before. I might end up looking real pissed off and not just fake-angry. Then he might look at Annie, release the dancers from his eyes and go, "Whoa, men-in-white-coat time. Crazy cousin."

Besides, even if I could manage the right voice, my bathing suit's unhooked, and what if I stood up too fast before the hook was secured and the top fell down? I glance over at

Leslie to see if she's going to say something funny, but she's taking some sandwiches out of her backpack and putting them on a little plate.

"Maybe" pops out of my mouth. "Maybe you can also put a sandwich on my back and a can of Coke so that at the end of the day, I'll have shapes of a whole lunch there."

His eyes open a little wider as if he didn't expect me to say that. He doesn't look angry at all for a moment. Instead, he cracks up and shows perfect teeth. "How about some fries? We could make a happy face right here." He touches the center of my back with his finger, making two dots for eyes and a swipe for the smile.

Cool waves run from where his finger touches me, turning into a wild heat that flashes between my legs and makes me unbearably ashamed and exhilarated. I want to run down into the ladies' locker room, catch my breath and just think about this over and over and over. I need to look in the mirror at my back and see if the places he touched are highlighted with dark brown sparkles.

I laugh nervously and my ears hear a giggle come out of my own mouth that's like one Annie would do. Then there's the sound of someone pulling the tab open on a can of soda and at the same time Eva says, "How's that arm, Andrew?"

There's a shifting of bodies next to me. Leslie moves closer to my head so that Eva can sit next to Andrew. I watch Eva's profile as she looks at his cast, as if she could see how the bones are healing beneath it.

"You tell me, doc, how am I doing?" he says.

She rolls her eyes. "I wish you guys would stop calling me that. I haven't made up my mind yet."

Even from my side view of her I can see the glints of pleasure sparking out of her eyes. The others have gathered around as Leslie lays out more food, and I can tell Eva's glad they're all hearing about her tentative reluctance to acknowledge the gifts of her superior intellect. Then her eye-glints stop as Andrew slides the Dorito to the right side of my back and says, "I think it looks better here."

Eva turns from his arm to glare at me. I feel a new wave of hate coming from her, climbing higher and higher, arching to crash over my head and send me whirling into the deep end of the ocean, with all of them watching from shore.

She reaches across Andrew, making sure her hair brushes against his shoulder, and takes a Dorito. She bites a tiny corner off of it and turns to him. "I mean, who could possibly have decided what they want to do with their lives by now? Although, I guess if you had, like, a special gift, you would know."

Nobody picks up her cue to mention her special gift for science and math. She nibbles another crumb from the Dorito and her eyes flash over the group. Annie, magically no longer on the diet she decreed we were on at breakfast, is eating some fries someone brought up from the snack bar downstairs. JKIII has picked up a half of one of Leslie's sandwiches. Eva waits until there is a silence, broken only by the sounds of chewing, then says, "Hey, Stephanie, have you thought about teaching fifth grade or something? It'd be perfect, you know, cuz you're so small. The kids would feel safe with you." She giggles. "Couldn't you just see the kids, you guys? They walk into class the first day, see Stephanie and say, 'Hey, where's the teacher?' "

She laughs really hard and I have no idea who else is joining in because I feel such a deep rumbling in my brain, I know an earthquake is happening there and all my Warrior Words from the countless hours of my lonely reading are bursting free. They slide down from my brain to my mouth. By the time the words get to my tonsils, they are old friends in battle gear. They are finally ready to come forward. They are ready to help me, waving flags and hoisting Uzis.

"Actually," I say in a dead calm voice, "I'm being conscripted into what could generally be considered the global, Boston-Irish-Catholic family business. The typical ontogeny recapitulating phylogeny situation. Not that I mind. I'm actually thrilled about one day becoming a senator. I like the idea of fighting for egalitarianism. Could you imagine, Eva, the socioeconomic repercussions of a return to say, primogeniture?"

I keep my eyes opened in concerned inquiry. My heart is pounding. Eva freezes with a Diet Coke to her lips. Though I stare at her, I can see Andrew, Leslie, Annie and JKIII out of the corner of my eye, hazy colors with tanned, startled expressions on top. First, they find out I'm a Facebook rebel and now this. No one says a word, and without looking around, I can feel all the eyes weaving into one big question directed at Eva. She's the batter up, the big-talking slugger who's now at the plate.

She lowers her hand, setting her drink down, and looks at me. For a moment I almost feel sorry for her as fear skitters in her eyes like lizards suddenly illuminated by headlights at the side of a desert road. She coughs slightly, then says with as much interested concern as she can muster, "No, uh, no, I can't."

I close my eyes, nesting my chin in the soft comfort of my towel. My mind explodes with fragments of words flashing like fireworks, tumbling down onto my eyelids. Sounds of crackling chip bags and rustling bodies float up to my ears, gradually easing the tight band between my shoulder blades. Through the blind haze of suntan lotion, fries and far-off cigarette smoke, Andrew's cologne of anger and despair seeps into my body, and I shudder against my towel in terror and longing.

CHAPTER SEVEN

Someone is barbecuing. Meat singes the air. There's a prick of coolness on the breeze as the sun slants low, splintering its light through the high leaves of the trees, which wave slightly, unhurried and uninvolved, above us.

I can't believe that this is only my second night in L.A. and the fourth day since my mom left. I feel like I've lost all concept of real time. Like I'm a time traveler from another world and everything that happened to me in Boston could have been years ago. I focus only on what is happening here. I keep all the Boston thoughts and memories in a little capsule in the middle of my spine, away from my heart and away from my brain, so I don't have to feel or think about any of it.

I keep thoughts about my mom buried the deepest. About a hundred times a day, images of her ping up into my head. Sometimes they're good images and sometimes they're bad. Sometimes she's brushing my hair and my heart aches for her so much I can't breathe. Other times, she's my evil mother, the one of striking fists and raging eyes.

In the same minute, I can have ten images of each kind blasting in my head and battling with each other to find out which is the real her. When these battles wage, I feel exhausted and empty, as if it sucks out all my guts having two fighting mothers inside me.

Sometimes, I think about sneaking a ride to the airport and stowing away on a plane so I can fly back to Boston and comb the streets for her. I feel like I must have a secret power inside because I'm her daughter. That the power would pull her to me, no matter how drunk she was when I found her. That she could even be blindfolded but would rush over when she heard my voice, like a mother cow hearing her calf in the middle of a great herd.

Then I think, Where was my big, secret power when she

was standing right in front of me? Where was it when she pried my hands from around her waist and took off into the rain?

I can't even call her since, of course, she doesn't have a cell phone. Maybe she was even thinking of ditching me then, the day I asked her if we could both get them.

I haven't been able to talk to my dad either. I left a message for him when I first landed. Then, Uncle Michael said he called back while we were at the club.

My dad said he was going to send me a cell phone when I got out here so we could have long chats about my adventures. He said it when he was driving me to the airport and his eyes were still runny and I wasn't really speaking to him. Now I don't even want him to send me one. First, it would never be one like the kids have out here, and second, it would ruin my whole Facebook rebel story.

Who cares about him anyway?

I touch my spine, feel a little ridge, and am glad that the capsule of Boston is staying tightly closed.

I look over at Leslie, who is doing an imitation of an old man with a long nose who works at the pro shop at the club and always says, "Ladies, ladies, may I help you," with a tiny lisp on the *s*. Andrew sits next to me in shorts and a baseball shirt that's white in the middle and blue on the arms. His hair is slightly damp from the bike ride into the woods. Guy sweat seeps from him in a tangy fragrance, threatening to pull something wild out of me that I never knew was there.

We've all ridden from the club to the spot in the woods at Mulholland where we were last night. We're in a circle around a flashlight bonfire. Everyone is sitting cross-legged except for Annie, who's leaning against JKIII's chest with his legs on either side of her. His hands are rubbing the patch of her stomach between her shirt and her shorts.

Everyone's been asking me questions about my life in Boston. I'm unaccustomed to this much attention, but I've already learned from watching Eva talk about her math and science award that I should appear reluctant to discuss myself. So at first I protest that nothing I do is very interesting, and then I spit out a string of lies, one at a time, like a rainbow of glass beads. Once the lies are out, they grow arms and legs and silent, stoic faces that guard my secrets of unwashed hair, stale snacks from greasy boxes, and cold walks home from school in shoes that have long been too tight. The lies surround me with their golden shields and ice-tipped spears, letting no one look in and see my motherless life.

I've painted myself as a distant cousin of the Kennedys,

not by blood but by friendship. I've told everyone how we all rallied around Ted Kennedy when he came out strongly for Obama, making it sound like my family was there at brunches and dinners, having intense, high-powered political discussions.

I've got my family playing football on the Cape, laughing as they stumble into each other, with big kids tossing little kids into the air. Even as the stories spill straight from the stored-up pages of my mother's Kennedy books, I truly smell the fresh salt air of Hyannis Port and feel the grit of the football upon my palms and the trembling freedom as I run toward a touchdown.

Lastly, I cut off any future scrutiny into my lack of new, cute outfits by telling them how it's so different with the old East Coast families and people would rather hang themselves than be caught wearing anything trendy. I let my shabby clothes somehow speak of my understated, blueblood pedigree.

Even Eva seems spellbound, sitting the farthest from me but staring almost unblinking with her black, glittering eyes.

In addition to everyone who was hanging out on the sundeck at the club there's also another guy who met us here. A guy named Carl who's almost as tall as Andrew and has braces and isn't cute or athletic at all. He's sort of like the servant of the guys' group. Like normally he wouldn't even get to hang out with them, but they need someone to fetch for them so he's worth having around. Now there are five guys to five girls, but no one's a couple except for Annie and JKIII.

I think Emily, whom I still think of as a sleepy peach, likes Brian. He's sitting across from her with his shirt off and she keeps looking at him, opening her usually dreamy eyes more than usual, as if finally, there is something to wake up for.

At first I was thinking that Leslie didn't like anyone since she kind of acts like the mom, always bringing out food and calling the guys by their last names, as if there's nothing wild inside of her that she needs to be afraid of. Then, I remember that she hooked up with some guy named Ben and I see her differently, her breasts not a mother's but a girl's.

I have no doubt whom Eva likes. She watches everything Andrew does and I see him through her eyes: his hand that for one second touched my knee and his eyes that flicker over my legs while I tell the story about my parents waiting white-faced with the Kennedy family while the Coast

Guard searched icy waters for John Jr. when his plane went down.

During all of my tales, Annie keeps her eyes on me as if I were an old necklace she found in a drawer and didn't expect to like, only to discover that with a little rub, I became an opal, shooting iridescent sparks into her whirling light, making her even more blinding.

After a while, I refuse to answer any more questions, insisting I'd just bore them. When I say this, Andrew tosses a rock that tears a leaf off of a tree and says, "Senator, you're anything but boring."

Annie immediately pounces on my new title, as it only adds to her own luminescence. Every time she addresses me now, it's as "Senator" and so, of course, the other girls do it too. All except Eva. She makes a point of calling me Stephanie in a tight, precise voice, as if the power of her authoritative tone will steer everyone back to calling me only by my name.

Brian says, "I've thought about politics," and tosses a rock higher than Andrew's and looks satisfied when we hear a little thwack.

Andrew says, "If you want to go into politics, you'd better

recapitulate her philosophy or whatever the hell she said," and grabs another stone.

While he and Brian fight for dominance, throwing rocks higher and higher against the tree, Annie says, "Mind your manners" to JKIII in that schoolteacher voice she and Leslie use. Leslie starts packing up snacks and cigarettes in her backpack and I know it's time to go.

As we stand, I want to freeze the moment and hold on to it like the snow on Christmas Eve, when each ice crystal shimmers in expectation, hiding the fact that Santa is really my mom, who'll be in bed all of Christmas Day, still drunk from the rum in the eggnog, splayed half naked on her bed, with smeared lipstick and clumps of hairsprayed hair hanging down, like someone's bad idea of ornaments.

• • •

I have a new name for Aunt Sarah: The Digester. At dinner, she passes up the roast chicken, mashed potatoes and bread only to heap endless servings of salad and vegetables on her plate until I picture her, an hour after dinner, lying glazed in front of the television set, thin like a snake but for the enormous bulge around her middle.

Uncle Michael eats with perfectly cut bites, pausing between them to tell stories and ask questions. He never looks as if he's hungry, just as if eating were something interesting to do while he has a conversation. I wish I could blink and he would be my father, Carson Drew, and we could be with Chief McGinnis from the River Heights Police force, who would shake his head and say, kind of marveling at me, "Stephanie, just how did you determine the painting was a forgery?"

An elbow jabs me in the ribs. "Can you believe how he's eating?" Annie hisses. "He's such a pig."

I look over in the direction where she's staring. Her brother Patrick is shoving a huge bite of chicken into a mouth already brimming with mashed potatoes. Annie takes a tiny bite from the tip of her fork. "They are so gross," she says furiously. "Don't you dare tell anyone how they eat."

I feel a blast of rage. This is all she has to be horrified about? This is her dark secret? Jealousy claws at my chest. I want her life so badly I could tear her face off with my bare hands and plaster my own over her network of blood and veins if I thought it would be a successful way for us to trade places.

At the other end of the table by Aunt Sarah, Megan spills

her milk. Subconsciously, I brace myself for hollering and blows. Megan starts to cry as the milk trickles down her leg and Aunt Sarah only says, "Shush, honey, it's okay. It just scared you."

Carmen comes and cleans up the mess. Immediately, a new milk is set in front of Megan, who still sniffles like a victim. I hate Megan all over again, and so I look over at Michael Jr. and try to hear what he's saying to Daniel. I pick up the words *unbe-LIEV-ably hot.*

Aunt Sarah doesn't hear this because she's too busy telling Megan how proud of her she is for holding her new milk like a good girl. The expression hasn't escaped Annie though, who sets her eyes upon her brothers like lasers and demands, "Who? Who is?"

Daniel says, "None of your beeswax."

Patrick, with more mashed potatoes in his mouth, says to his brother in complete wonder, "You met her?"

Now everyone's focusing on their conversation. Annie says scornfully, "Who, some stupid actress?"

Michael Jr. now addresses the whole table but mostly his father. "New family, bought the Taylors' house. Just moved here from Georgia. Some kind of crazy Arab last name—"

"Michael." Aunt Sarah flashes him an angry teacher look.

Michael Jr. ignores her. "I met their daughter at the club today. James Mattson got them a guest pass. He wants to sponsor them as members—"

"Really," Aunt Sarah says, no longer the angry teacher, but a club member excited to be the bearer of fresh gossip for her girlfriends.

"Oh, I heard about them," Uncle Michael cuts in. "The father's supposed to be some sort of genius in chemistry—all the pharmaceuticals were fighting over him."

Michael Jr. doesn't seem the least bit interested in the genius father. He leans over to Patrick and whistles softly. "What's truly a crime is, the daughter is only fourteen."

"Get out," Patrick says. "May the Lord strike me dead. Or at least blind."

Daniel punches him in the arm and they do a mini-wrestle at the table. I'm distracted for a moment until I realize that Annie is tensing beside me. "Who is she?" she says with a huff of sheer boredom, but I recognize the tone. It's the same one she uses when anyone at the pool admires a model in a magazine. She asks to see the picture as if she couldn't care less, then she scrutinizes it with her breath coming out her nose in harsh, tiny puffs. When she finds what she's looking for, something wrong with the model, like too-thin lips or too wide of a forehead, she shouts out her discovery and makes everyone agree. On the one occasion where she couldn't find anything wrong, she tossed the magazine back at Emily and said, "Jesus, do you realize how much makeup they put on these girls? She'd probably look like hell if you just ran into her shopping or something."

"I think her name is Amal," Michael Jr. continues. "As they used to say in your day, Dad, 'foxy.'"

"Amal," Annie says scornfully, but it's drowned out by her brothers' laughter. I laugh too, just to be in on it, until I feel Annie seething beside me. I stop laughing and take a tiny peek at her. She's hunched over her plate, spearing a green bean, but with her mouth closed like a gate so I know she's not going to eat it. When she screeches her chair back to indicate she's through, I wonder what blood lies ahead as she prepares to enter prettiest-girl battle.

• • •

Annie's texting furiously as I walk by her room. Her face is tight and she doesn't even notice me go by. I finally have the opportunity I've been praying for. I walk out onto the patio where Uncle Michael reads through the parts of the paper he didn't have time to touch in the morning.

The clatter of Carmen doing the dishes and Aunt Sarah reading to Megan is behind me as I slip out the double doors. Uncle Michael takes a sip of his drink and looks up at me. "So where are you two hooligans running off to tonight?"

I shrug. "Not sure yet. Annie's still on the phone. I was just hoping to catch up on the paper. Mind if I take a section?"

His eyebrows shoot up in surprise and then he catches himself. "Which one?"

I sit stiffly on one of the green chairs across from him. "Are you done with the front page?"

He takes a sip of his drink, and I'm nervous because I think he's laughing at me and trying to hide it. "Or, any other section is fine," I add, quickly looking off at the wide spread of trees, as if some small animal caught my attention.

"No, I'm done with the front section." He hands it to me. "Anything in particular that interests you?"

I consider tossing out my newly designed senatorial aspirations of the afternoon, but then I fear I'll be asked questions about things that I know nothing about. "Law," I say decisively. "I love any stories about legal stuff."

His face brightens like I just put a surprise birthday cake in front of him and told him it was his turn to blow out the candles. "Really? You know, I was already interested in the law at your age too."

He tells me a story about when he was fifteen and he heard about a man getting his leg smashed in a car accident and the drunken driver refused to pay for all the days he missed at work.

"That did it for me," he says. "Right then and there, I decided to be a lawyer."

I'm listening as hard as I can, hoping that he'll feel just how interested I am. At the same time though, I'm trying to figure out how to ask the big question. I wish he would tell another story so I'd have more time to think, but he's looking at me now as if it's my turn to speak. Since I have no game plan I just blurt out, "Maybe I could work for you? Like help you with your cases? But, um, for free, of course."

I'm blushing profusely now at the thought that maybe he thought I wanted him to pay me money.

I can't look at his eyes because I'm so embarrassed, so I stare at his temple, thinking that it's the exact amount of gray Carson Drew has. He frowns and clears his throat.

"And what kind of work would you want to do?" he asks, and his mouth tightens at the sides like he's holding in a huge laugh.

I'm about to cry and know I could never tell him that I want to actually solve cases with him, that my childish dream of solving "mysteries" has matured into a real passion to work on real law stuff. I just shrug and blink really fast so the tears dry before they spill out.

"Well," he says in a serious voice. "Let me give it some thought."

Annie runs out onto the patio and all of a sudden I realize that in the back of my ear, I've been hearing her call me for the last couple of minutes. She stops dead in her tracks when she sees me sitting right across from her dad with my face all red. "You coming or not?" she says. Her voice has none of its usual hey-cousin friendliness.

I get up from my chair, and as we walk through the laundry room and into the garage, I see Uncle Michael's briefcase sitting next to the back door. While we get on our bikes, the idea sparks. Maybe I can get into his briefcase, see what kind of case he's working on and figure it out on my own? My favorite teacher at school, Sister Margaret, used to say, "Just because you're young doesn't mean you're wrong." Maybe that's what I can show him I could bring to the table, a fresh perspective.

I smile as we pedal up to Mulholland, picturing his face, creased with an incredulous smile, standing with me, my dad and somehow my mom saying, "And this little dickens figured out the money was counterfeit all by herself."

I descend back into reality when my bike hits a bump. I realize that Annie's been talking nonstop since we left the house and is now saying, "I don't know if I'll ever speak to him again. As far as I'm concerned, we're totally broken up."

• • •

Our cigarettes glow red against the black night. The guys aren't here yet, so the girls have all had time to hear Annie's story about what a jerk JKIII was on the phone. When she asked him if he had met the new girl, Amal, he had said, "Who, that really hot chick? Yeah, my parents invited her and her parents over for dinner last night."

Annie goes on to describe how she first acted as if she didn't hear him say that and just said, "So what's she like?" And then he had the unbelievable nerve to call her hot again. Like her hotness wasn't an opinion but an established fact. Like she was some sort of well-known Hollywood bombshell. At which point Annie told him that maybe things weren't working out anymore, and when he'd asked her why, she'd said, "Just because." But what she was really thinking was, Duh!

I watch the other girls to see what we're supposed to do. First, they all look at her like it's really bad news, like somebody's in the hospital. I mirror their expressions and remember a cat I found and put a rope around his neck so he wouldn't run away and who was strangled by morning, so that I'll be sure to look sad enough.

Leslie calls him a bastard and Emily just keeps saying "Unbelievable" at everything Annie says. Eva blows her smoke through her nose and says, "Maybe it's time for a little Bump Around tonight?"

Annie gives her first smile of the night and I have a new glimpse of Eva's role in the whole organization. Before I came, she sat at the right hand of Annie, the thinker, the idea friend. The unemotional one who could still steer the ship in the storm.

"Absolutely," Annie says, and before I have a chance to ask about Bump Around, flashlights hit our eyes and Andrew,

Brian, Matt and Carl walk up. With them is a stocky guy with blond hair named Ben, and without even looking at Leslie, I know her face has brightened and her breasts will point to and zoom in on this boy who she's already hooked up with.

Nobody mentions JKIII and I have no idea if Brian even knows about his big brother's breakup. Andrew walks over to say "Hey" to me. I don't know what's acceptable protocol in terms of what type of information we're allowed to tell the boys, but suddenly I feel so nervous that I just say, "Did you know Annie and JKIII broke up?"

"Huh." He shakes his head, then adds, "He's playing tennis with Ralph tonight."

I have no idea who Ralph is, but Leslie asks me if I want a cig and I nod so that when she tosses me one, I just grab it and put it into my mouth.

Before anyone even throws me a lighter, Andrew takes the cigarette out of my mouth and says, "Don't smoke tonight."

I'm totally confused. All the girls are smoking so I know it's the cool thing to do. None of the guys smoke though, except for Matt, so maybe they don't think it's cool.

Andrew says, "Don't look so worried, Senator," and a whiff of his breath hits me and I think in a blinding flash, What if he's planning on kissing me?

I'm burning with red, so I quickly drop my eyes and act like I have something under my nail. He clears his throat and I know he's still looking at me. I panic and drop my hand since he probably thinks I'm gross, like what do I do, pick my nails all day?

Annie stamps out her cigarette and says, "Bump Around, anyone?"

The girls giggle. The guys hit each other. Andrew looks at me and says, "Why not."

Eva catches his look and glares at me while Annie announces, "John and I broke up, I just want everyone to know."

The guys don't act all sorry or ask what happened. Matt looks straight at Annie like maybe now he'll have a shot. I'm glad nobody has a crush on Matt because they would be hurt by the way his eyes suck up Annie's hair and boobs and legs.

Eva stares at me like I'm that frog in biology again, and then says, as if she's not staring right at me, "Annie, does your cousin know how to play?"

I kind of shake my head slightly, flickers of terror striking across my chest. I'm glad the night hides my face.

Annie sees my head shake and says, "No."

"Perfect," Eva says. "Then she can go first."

The girls giggle again. The guys shove and push each

other and form a loose ring. The night heaves around me in thick puffs of black broken by patches of colored clothing where someone's careless hand glides a flashlight across the different bodies. I don't know what to expect. My heart thunders. I know something sexual is about to happen. I want to beg not to go first, but I want so badly to belong to this group that thinks I'm going to be a senator and doesn't know of my mother's whiskey breath and bloodshot eyes.

Eva steps into the middle of the circle of guys, ties a bandanna around my eyes and starts to spin me. Her hands are bony on my shoulders, and I think of a strange bird that's half witch. I'm getting dizzier and dizzier as my tennis shoes stumble around in the dirt.

"Okay," she says in a whisper, then takes her hands off my shoulders. I feel her leave my side as if the air opened up and took her thin, vibrating presence to a dark canyon beneath the earth. "Walk," her voice says from far away. "Walk."

I take a step and lurch to the right. Big hands hold me up. Guy hands.

"Take her blindfold off. Take it off."

I think the voice is Leslie's, but I'm so paralyzed with fear that I can't be sure. Hands push the blindfold up rather than untying it. I'm staring straight at a chest in a white T-shirt.

My head is still spinning and I lose my balance for a second and fall forward. The voice above the shirt goes, "Whoa."

I look up. Shadows dance across a face broken by the glint of metal on teeth. Braces. It's Carl. He hunches his shoulders and reaches his face in toward me. Before I can analyze what's happening, he's pressing his lips on mine. I realize I'm in a kiss and I can smell suntan lotion and taste salt at the same time. I wonder if this is all there is to it and how long it will go on when he pushes back from me and I realize it's over.

Annie goes next, then Emily and Leslie. No one's fallen into Andrew yet, and when it's Eva's turn, she giggles like she's one of the other girls and not a winner of a science and math award. Annie spins Eva and then lets her go. Eva takes two steps to the right, then acts like she's falling to the left and lands right into Andrew. She must have been peeking. He pushes up her blindfold and leans his head forward to press his lips onto hers.

I feel like someone just hit me in the stomach with a huge tree branch, and the same tears that never got to fall on the patio with Annie's dad brim up again. I shove them into the capsule in my spine and hope they'll stay until I can get out of here.

Finally, we're on our bikes and I'm grateful for the night on the way home, the way the darkness hugs my sides and hides my face. My legs pedal hard, blurs of pale yellow pants gleaming like stolen bits of moonlight. My bike floats. To my right, thousands of lights shimmer in the valley. There's a richness around me, a thick, mysterious fragrance of longing.

Sweat slips out of my hair and cools on my face. Annie yells, "Hey, wait up," but I don't slow down. The wind is my only friend, drying the tears that crept up from my spine and into my eyes before they have a chance to fall.

I arrive at the tall, arched walls of Annie's house. I think of flying past it, riding down the hill to Ventura Boulevard and then out to the shadowy parts of the Valley, where I would run into a down-and-out private investigator who would look me over, pull his cigar out of his mouth and say, "Okay, kid, you're hired. One week for starters." Then he'd slap a huge file into my hand and I'd be off, tracking down a woman hidden in a nursing home, concealing her true identity by acting like she has amnesia.

Instead, I turn up Annie's long driveway and a minute later she pulls up out of breath. "Hel-lo," she says irritably. "It wasn't a race."

I look at her like I don't get that she's pissed. "Oh, sorry. I thought you were right next to me."

We go into the garage and park our bikes against the wall. Even in her sweat she is stunningly beautiful. She pulls the barrette out of her hair and says, "Could you believe Eva? There's no way she wasn't peeking. She's had a crush on Andrew for, like, ages."

"Huh." I shrug as if I hadn't even noticed and keep walking into the house.

She tries again. "What was with Matt? I thought he was going to suck out Leslie's tonsils. I think he definitely got some tongue action in, don't you?"

I'm suddenly too tired for her world that's too old, too beautiful, and too unattainable for me. I only want to huddle under my blankets, push her and all her friends out of my brain, and be bathed by my words.

We walk up the stairs. I blink away the hot tears that pulse up again. In the darkness I see my mother walking into the rain, not even turning to say good-bye. I suddenly ache to see her, to tell her about my night.

"Well, good night," Annie says when we get to her bedroom door, in a voice cold with disappointment.

I want to scream into her face, What do you want from me? What? I go into my room and slip on the pajamas that already went through two cousins and are a faded pink and totally ugly, but soft as air.

I turn to the bed, ready to bury myself in its layers, and let my words flutter around me, over and over, until they whirl me into sleep. I'm just about to pull the covers back when I see a note on my pillow that my dad left a message on the kitchen answering machine. A tingling starts in my spine that goes straight to the backs of my eyes with a pulsing of unshed tears.

I run downstairs, into the kitchen, and freeze. Annie and her mom stand at the granite island. Annie is scooping ice cream into two bowls and her mother is saying, "Just a smidge," clearly digressing from her mounds of vegetation eating. They both look at me at the same time and I see my ancient, shapeless pajamas mirrored in their eyes before they both quickly blink. Obviously, my story about old East Coast families not buying trendy clothes can only go so far. No one would wear these pajamas if they had another choice. Maybe now Annie is going to start wondering what's really the story with me.

All of it further exhausts me.

Annie stays cool, focusing on the ice cream and still irritated with me while her mom summons a friendly smile and says, "Oh, did you come down to hear your dad's message?"

Annie's eyebrows shoot up. Obviously, she's remembering what I told her about being a Facebook rebel. I can tell by her face that she's torn between acting friendly with me again and staying mad because I didn't give her enough attention on the way home.

While I'm thinking about whether I should say something friendly to her to make up for the way home, Aunt Sarah walks over to the answering machine on the kitchen counter and presses a button, explaining as she goes. "It's really simple. Probably like one you have at home. Just hit 'play' when the light is blinking." I'm horrified that she would press the button publicly instead of letting me do it in private when she and Annie have left.

I don't even have time to prepare before my dad's voice floats into the spacious kitchen, leaky and unsure. "Hey, kiddo. Just hoping to catch you, but I guess it's hard with the time change and all. Okay, well, be good. I guess I have to catch you later."

Aunt Sarah hits "erase" and all traces of him are gone.

I'm left standing in the kitchen with the capsule of rage no longer held in my spine but racing up into my heart and exploding.

That's it? That's it?

That's *all*?

My breath is coming out in short puffs and I know I have to get out of this kitchen. NOW.

I turn to leave, but Aunt Sarah and Annie with their mother-daughter bowls of ice cream stand between me and my escape up the stairs.

Aunt Sarah looks at me with concern. My lower lip quivers and I pray with everything I've got: God, please don't let her speak. If she says one nice thing to me, I won't be able to keep pretending that everything's fine. I'll burst into tears and then Annie will know I'm just a mutt. A mutt with matted fur, dumped on her doorstep with nobody who cares about it, no one who's out scouring the neighborhood to bring it home and back into the hearth of the family who loves it.

With a push of strength from somewhere deep down inside me, I choke out a quick and carefree "Night," then run with splinters of rage, erupting like fireworks, into my soft and tastefully decorated bedroom.

CHAPTER EIGHT

I lie in bed in a ball, finally alone, letting the storm of tears fall. I cry in great, heaving blasts. There are no Warrior Words that can help me now. They're all just struggling and looking at me angrily, like I should have known they could only do so much. That they could protect me only from things outside me, not things inside.

Thoughts of my dad merge into thoughts of my mom, rising up like tiny spikes to stab the few good memories in my brain. The memories bleed in great, red waterfalls, turning into salty oceans as they pour out of my eyes as tears.

After my last shuddering breath is the part I hate even more. The wide, open emptiness, when I'm spent and hollow.

I hold my hand up to my hair on my head and think coldly, Why brush it anyway? I picture my mom for one moment more, her dark hands soft on my hair, her face reflected above mine in my bedroom mirror, where her eyes smiled into mine.

It hurts more to think about her than about my dad, so I focus on him. How weak he is and how disgusted I am with him. Then it hurts just as much to think of him, so I start thinking about Annie's dad and longing throbs at my temples like a steady drum. I let myself slip back into the moment on the porch when Uncle Michael told me about how he decided to become a lawyer and how he didn't laugh when I asked him if I could work for him and he said he'd give it some thought.

I remember his briefcase with growing excitement, and I think now is my chance. I can impress him beyond his wildest dreams. I can become a mini junior partner at his firm and Annie won't even be jealous because all she cares about is clothes and boys so I can still have her as a friend and a cousin.

I creep to my door and open it. Darkness heaves, making the hall seem narrower.

I walk as straight and steady as an ant. When I get to the top of the stairs I almost turn back, but instead bite on my lip and descend. In the foyer I pause and listen for noise, but there's nothing. I press my arms to my chest to hold in a shiver and then step, quiet as dust, into the family room.

Pale light from around the pool floats onto the floor, showing shadowy crisscrosses from the lattice outside on the patio. My bare feet rise and fall on the cold tiles, and then I'm in the laundry room. I sneak ahead until I bump into the smooth leather of Uncle Michael's briefcase.

I'm afraid to turn on any light, but I won't be able to do what I have to do if I can't see. There's a refrigerator in the laundry room and I figure that if I slide the door to the room closed, the light from the opened refrigerator door won't be too obvious.

While I have the refrigerator open, I realize I'm thirsty and pretty tired so I open a can of Coke for the caffeine. I slurp down a little and then focus on the briefcase. It's deep brown leather with gold clasps. I don't think they're locked because I've seen Uncle Michael go in and out of it and have never seen him use a little key.

I press the gold buttons out to the side and hear a faint click. Excitement beats in my chest and I cross my fingers before I open the top. The case he's working on is all in folders. I'm not sure which document to start with so I just take the one off the top. It says "Interrogatories." I start reading, waiting to hear the story of who wants what. I'd rather look for a person than an heirloom or something, but I'll take what I can get.

What I'm reading must not be connected to the case because it just has numbers that keep asking for things I don't understand. Maybe it's just some kind of legal bill. I take a long sip of my Coke. The next document is something I don't understand either. I dig down farther to find pictures of the missing person or the lost jewels.

I've gotten to the bottom of the briefcase. Things are not working out. There are no pictures here at all. I grab another manila envelope to look through and my Coke falls right onto the "Interrogatories." Soda gushes out.

I'm in so much shock that it takes me a minute to move. Then I pick up the can and hurry out toward the kitchen to get some paper towels. I think I hear a noise from upstairs so I immediately stop my mouth breath and just suck in tiny bits of air through my nose. I try to make my nostrils tiny slits like this old woman's I saw in church. I wait with my knife-cut nostrils until I'm sure no one is coming down from upstairs.

I start moving again and steal into the kitchen. I have a little light from the moon outside so I fumble around until I finally hit a shadowy roll of paper towels. I grab a bunch of them and then hurry back into the laundry room.

I hear a toilet flush from upstairs so I'm afraid to open the refrigerator door in case the person upstairs will notice a sliver of light. I just wipe frantically in the dark, my heart pounding with fear. The pages are soaked and have already started to get bumps in them. I wipe harder and harder, hoping that somehow I'm getting it all. When it feels dry, I close the briefcase and put it back exactly where it was. I stuff the wet paper towels in the trash under the sink and creep out of the laundry room and up the stairs.

I crawl back into bed and lie there with my hand on my chest, pushing down on my skin, trying to get my heart to stop pounding. I try to sleep but just seem to twist and turn for hours, dread keeping me awake, hearing, just as I start to drift, the small click of the briefcase as the golden latches click open.

CHAPTER NINE

I have no idea what time it is, but I can tell it's late because I can hear Annie screaming, "Eeeww, these blueberries are moldy." She never gets up before ten so it must be after that. I had thought maybe I would get up early and confess about the briefcase, but by now Uncle Michael will be long gone. I push away pictures of him in a nice wood-paneled office with all his diplomas behind him on the wall, opening up his briefcase to find those sticky papers. I'm starting to hope that maybe he won't need to go in it all day, or maybe, since I wiped up all the Coke, they really won't be sticky, just a little wrinkled and he won't even notice.

I throw on some shorts and a shirt and go downstairs. Annie stares out at the patio while she spears watermelon from a glass bowl like she hates each piece. I try to think of a girl comment, like something Leslie would say. Nothing comes to mind until I remember Annie's broken up with JKIII so I say, "You still bummed about John?"

She brightens just a spot as if she'd given up on me as a girlfriend last night but now thinks maybe I was just tired. Daniel and Patrick lumber by with surfboards and faded sweatshirts, and Annie leans forward to keep our conversation exclusive. I feel a thrill whipping out through the end of my fingertips. I am, for a moment, at the epicenter of belonging. I am the queen's confidant.

"He left a message on my cell last night. I would have played it for you, but you, like, ran up the stairs when my mom and I were getting ice cream." She flips her hair over her shoulder and purses her lips into a slight pout so I can be reminded of how I failed her.

I lower my head slightly, remorseful for ignoring the queen's needs.

"Anyway," she continues, "he said he was really sorry, and was I mad at him for making that bonehead comment about this new girl being so hot and did I want to play tennis today."

I help myself to a bowl of watermelon Carmen has silently put before me. I'm glad Annie hasn't declared it a diet day. I also take a cinnamon bun from the tray Carmen has left for us. "So, are you going to play tennis with him?"

She tosses her head back and smirks. "That's for me to know and him to keep guessing."

I take my first bite of the cinnamon bun. I've never tasted anything like this. For a second I'm almost dizzy with the succulence of the hot icing hitting the roof of my mouth, and I close my eyes and take another bite. When I open them, Annie is staring at me.

"In love with the cinnamon bun," she says rudely, and I'm horribly ashamed, as if it's obvious to her I've never sampled the likes of which rise so easily and plentifully on her table.

"They're just a little different here than at home," I say, dropping my bun as if it's poison. "Our housekeeper always uses a thicker frosting, like it has some kind of cheese in it."

She's not even paying any attention to me. I feel a desperate need for her to know that I'm not impressed with her cinnamon buns, for her to know I've had lots and lots of them. That my kitchen is fragrant in the morning with baking and sliced fruit, and not messy and sticky with stale gin and dirty ashtrays.

She's already stood up, and suddenly I'm afraid that if I open my mouth at all, I'll burst into tears, and how will I explain that?

She hurries out to the patio, where she grabs our bathing suits that are now dry and hang over a low brick wall in the spot between the purple and red vines. We walk into the garage and get on our bikes, and I notice Annie doesn't take her tennis racket.

We pedal fast, especially up the last hill to the club. For a second, my paralyzing anxiety descends again about putting on the bathing suit. Then I remember that everyone's already seen me in it and I'll just come up with more interesting stories about being a kind of Kennedy.

We lock our bikes at the rack. I follow Annie's quick walk inside the club. Gray clouds press over the pool, squeezing out the blue. Humidity curls the ends of my hair. A glint of cool sharpens the air, and goose bumps rise up on my arm from a slice of breeze.

It feels as if something dangerous might happen today, like maybe motorcycle boys will screech into the club and beat up Annie's rich-kid friends, or someone will get hit on the head just before they dive into the pool, and one of the moms will scream, "Does anyone know CPR?"

Annie grabs a Diet Coke from the snack bar so I do too, even though I like regular. We head up the redwood stairs. There are no adults on the sundeck today and music blasts like fists. We make our way to the far end of the deck where huge pines make a fragrant wall of green. I try to imitate Annie's walk, where her waist leads and her hips swing out. Eva and Emily are already lathered up with suntan lotion, lying on their towels. Leslie stands at the edge of the deck, tanned and plump in a white bikini, sneaking a cig.

I scan the boys, trying to act like I'm not. I see Andrew and I know my face is turning beet red, so I look away quickly and say, "Hi" to the first person I see. It turns out to be Carl. This is not good because I have a fake smile on my face and Carl could think I'm smiling at him because I kissed him last night in Bump Around and that I like him.

I lose the smile.

Annie and I drop our towels next to Emily and Eva. Brian and Matt are staring at the girls' backs, acting like they keep finding spots where the girls forgot to put suntan lotion, even though it's so cloudy they probably don't need it at all. Brian touches a total inner-thigh area on Emily and goes, "Yup, it's gonna fry. Maybe if I could just put a little lotion on it for you."

Emily squeals and swipes his hand away, and I hope by the end of the summer I'll be able to squeal like that.

Ben, the guy who did the finger thing with Leslie, comes up the sundeck and tosses her a bag of chips, and it's funny how it's cool to eat junk instead of meals when you're rich, but sad if you're poor and your mother burns any meal she tries to make because she's too drunk.

Leslie drops her cigarette onto the ground and steps on it with her sandal. It's brown with a little jewel strap and I figure it must have cost a couple hundred dollars. She picks up the cigarette butt and tosses it into the redwood garbage container, and then walks over to us with her fingers poking into Ben's shoulder like she's trying to see if he has a sunburn.

Ben has shaggy blond hair and plays air guitar. He gives Leslie a kiss right on the lips and says to her, "I gotta take a leak." When he gets to the stairs I ask Leslie if she thinks I should lie out first on my back or my stomach.

I'm waiting for her to examine the front and back of my legs like she did for Emily yesterday to compare the tans. Instead she just goes, "Whatever," and I feel humiliated and cheated, furious at Ben for diverting her attention from what I thought was trusted girl stuff.

Annie lies on her stomach and unhooks her bathing suit

top. A voice from behind us says, "Need help with the lotion?" and I don't have to turn to know it's JKIII.

"Stephanie will do it," Annie says loftily and I scuttle over to her like a trained puppy.

I pour out the lotion carefully, happier about my job when I see Eva looking over, irritated that she wasn't asked. I rub the white lotion on Annie's glistening skin until it is perfectly melded with her tan, an invisible armor against sunburn in case the sun comes out.

I use my thumb to push the little opening of the top of the lotion closed and Annie's lids drop, dismissing me. My face shows nothing of the slight as I fall onto my towel and rub lotion on the front of my legs.

I wanted to lie on my stomach to keep my chest shielded from view because it flattens out even more when I'm lying on my back, but no one has asked me if I need lotion on my back, and I don't know who to ask. No one ever asks Annie to put lotion on them, and I would eat glass before I asked Eva.

JKIII lies right on the deck next to Annie's head. It's obvious he wishes he could speak to her privately, but she clearly isn't done punishing him yet. I finish putting lotion on my stomach and arms, then lie back and close my eyes. I don't want to miss a word. The stakes are high; she already let him put his hand in her pants.

"So, did you get my message last night?" he asks.

"Um, I think I did. I didn't have my cell with me and I got home pretty late and there were, like, ten of them to listen to." Her voice is lazy, unconcerned. I wonder if I'll ever get to act like I don't like a boy I do like and who likes me back.

"I really miss you," he says in an even quieter voice. "I was hoping we could play tennis today," he continues when she doesn't say anything.

I feel movement beside me. She sits up. "Bummer, I didn't bring my racket," she says, then adds, "But I'm soooo thirsty. I'd love it if you got me another Diet Coke."

I'm dying to see the look on his face, and I can feel the other girls waiting for his reply. I lift my lids just a fraction so I can get a read on where the other boys are standing. I know vaguely that their ability to hear this conversation will weigh into his decision to comply. I do a full scan of the deck. None of the other guys could have heard Annie's request.

JKIII is silent for a minute. Annie, his prize, shimmers just out of reach, attainable only with his total submission in getting the Diet Coke. More clouds bunch in the sky while he weighs and considers. I already know what he will do.

"I'm totally parched," he announces getting to his feet. "Can I get any of you ladies anything?"

I open my eyes fully now and sit up. My "No, thanks" slides out of my throat, skipping up to him over Annie's face, which is beaming in a smile of the purest pleasure.

I pour more lotion into my hands because I want to look busy and not like I'm waiting for somebody to say something. Out of the corner of my eye I see Andrew walk over to our towels. I want to quickly lie back down and close my eyes so I can be lazy and disinterested if he says anything to me because of his kiss with Eva last night, but it's too late. He already saw my eyes looking at his.

When he stops in front of my towel and says, "Morning, Senator," I can't help but smile and say, "Hey."

I can't see Eva's face, but a bottle of lotion comes flying from her towel right at his chest. He catches it. "You're blocking my sun," she says to him.

He barely looks at her and just says, "Sorry," then drops down at the end of my towel. "You going to Mulholland tonight?" he asks me.

I have no clue how to flip my hair so I just shrug and keep my voice as Annie-like as possible. "Maybe."

He looks frustrated, like he thought I was going to say

something smart like I did the other day and instead I acted all girly. I'm totally confused so now I say in my normal voice, "Probably."

"Good," he says and does a friendly squeeze of my big toe like you would on a baby's cheek. "I'll see you there. I'm going to get my cast off right now."

He stands up and ambles off. My toe soars to the clouds, taking me with it, when Annie's voice cuts like diamonds, "*Who* is that?"

I turn to look in the direction she's looking. Two girls have come up the deck. One is not much taller than I am, sort of plain with long, dusty red hair. The other girl is as tall as Annie, and she is a dark goddess of unparalleled curves and bounty. They walk to our end of the sundeck and I can't take my eyes off of her breasts, which are winged and wide and fill up the front of her one-piece bathing suit in such an effulgence of fertility, I expect drums to be beaten and every male in the club to leap forward in worship.

No one in our group speaks. Annie looks like a shotgun went off in her face. I'm wildly glad Andrew isn't here. I hear Matt whisper, "Holy crap," and Emily looks like he slapped her.

The girls put down their towels. The redhead lies down

first on her stomach and unhooks her top. Everyone is silent as the goddess leans over her friend's back and pours lotion into small white pools. A groan escapes Matt when she starts to rub in the lotion in smooth, round strokes. Her breasts heave with her movement, stunningly attractive even though her suit is plain, boring and cut to cover as much of her body as possible.

When she's finished, she lies on her back and closes her eyes. Her double Everests settle only slightly at her sides, the majority of their bulk rising up so high that when I squeeze my eyes half shut, I see them blend with the clouds.

Even Annie is awestruck.

CHAPTER TEN

We didn't stay at the club very long. Annie said she was bored and that it was too cloudy to get any sun anyway. We ended up going shopping. Everyone bought clothes except for me. I just acted like I didn't like anything, because I didn't have any money. Now that we're home, Annie says she's exhausted and going to take a nap. I hear the TV in her room and her bustling around in front of her door where her mirror is, so I figure she's trying on all her new outfits.

I'm just glad she didn't ask me to watch her model them. There's a bookcase in my room and I really need to read.

I'm lying on the soft carpet, reading the titles on the

bottom shelf of the books, when there's a knock on my door. I sigh, waiting for Annie to blow in with yet another request to discuss the treachery of JKIII. "Ye-ah," I mutter halfheartedly. The door opens and Uncle Michael walks in stiffly. The briefcase is in his hand.

I sit up straight and swallow hard. His face is tight and closed, not like it was the last time I spoke to him, when we sat on the patio and talked about law.

He closes the door and faces me. I feel very small. Small and bad. Wrong at my core.

He opens up the briefcase and takes out a handful of bumpy, ruined documents. "I want you to tell me," he barks with no "hello" or anything, "what the hell you were up to." He is very, very angry, with a stranger's face. He is not at all Carson Drew.

I open my mouth wanting to be strong and own up to my mistake, but no sound comes out. Like my father, I'm passive in the face of an attack. I just look down, shame burning hotly through me.

My guilt is obvious. A hiss of disgust steams out of his mouth. I pull my knees up to make myself smaller.

"Look," he says harshly. "I owe a debt to your family and

I'm going to honor it. I'll pay to feed you and clothe you until your father can straighten out the mess he has going on in Boston. But the one thing I won't tolerate is you stealing from me, or anyone else in this house. Are we clear?"

"Stealing?" I mutter weakly and risk a quick glance at his face. I see him now as he must have always been, before I fastened my pathetic, father-hungry Carson Drew fantasy on him: a rich man living a smug, rich life with his smug, rich family.

I don't even try to defend myself. I'm just a crumb under the weight of his privileged righteousness. I hadn't even thought about the fact that he was paying for me to live there. I don't really even eat that much.

He turns and walks silently out the door.

I lie on my bed staring up at the ceiling. I'm too humiliated to even cry. There's another knock on my door and I steel myself for any comments he may have forgotten to make the first time.

Annie flies in, talking a mile a minute as usual. "Come on, I'm dying for a cig. And, I have some major new dish on that girl, Amal. Leslie's sister met her and said she's like really stupid."

I'm still lying there frozen. She slaps me in the leg. "Earth to Stephanie. Come. On."

She turns to go. I stare at her back dumbly. She turns around and glares at me, silent.

Somehow, my body gets up and I follow her downstairs and outside, praying that we won't run into her father. We don't run into anyone as we cross the patio and climb down some rocks to a path, about five feet below the yard, that winds around her property. We walk all the way to the back and break through some bushes. There are three big flat rocks in a semicircle totally enshrouded by green.

Annie sits down first and motions for me to sit on the rock next to her. She takes a pack of cigarettes out of the little purse she has over her shoulder. She hits the top of the pack expertly on the back of her hand and three cigarettes pop out ready for smoking. She lights hers first, then throws me one and the pack of matches. I'm still in shock so I just numbly light mine and clamp my teeth over the cough that lunges up from my throat.

Annie inhales deeply and throws her head back to make smoke rings above her head. Part of my brain is spinning, trying to think of how I can secretly call my father and beg him to fly me out tonight; the other part simply watches the way her mouth forms O's right before the smoke comes out.

She blows another smoke ring, then says, "Jesus, my cramps are killing me."

Her words hover above my head, mixing with the smoke. I can't really focus on her because I'm too preoccupied with the stark fear of running into her father later. I keep thinking that I should have said something, should have, at least, told him I wasn't stealing. But what could I have said—that I was looking for a case to solve? That I thought I could be Nancy Drew?

That I had wanted to make him my father?

Annie is looking at me now with what I recognize as her peevish pout since I haven't responded to her. I know I'd better say something, or, on top of everything, she'll know I haven't gotten my period, and if I still have to stay here, I can't have her knowing that.

"Midol's the best" flies out of my lips, and I'm glad I've seen the commercial with the concerned mom.

"Yeah, I'm out," she says, and I feel like I've just gotten away with a theft.

I'm about to try to make a smoke ring like she does so I

don't have to talk when Uncle Michael's voice comes from over our heads. "Isn't Carmen supposed to keep this clean?" Silently we both press our cigarettes into the ground.

Aunt Sarah says, "I'm sure she did it last Friday."

"That's not often enough," Uncle Michael answers in the new angry voice I heard tonight. The voice of the entitled stranger, used to nothing but the best, forced to deal with the incompetence or dishonesty of lesser beings.

Annie points up but I've already figured out that they're sitting in the gazebo, practically right over our heads.

We hear the tinkle of ice. Annie presses her hand over her mouth not to laugh. If the ugliness hadn't happened in my room, this would be one of those moments I've always dreamed of, girlfriends spying on the adults. Instead, I'm filled with dread.

"I wanted to come out here," Uncle Michael says, "so the kids wouldn't hear."

Annie raises her eyebrows in a face like, tell-us-more. I think I can guess what's coming. I frantically motion for us to go, but she swats at my arm, like, are-you-out-of-your-mind?

"I think she may be a bad influence on Annie," Uncle Michael opens.

We both know whom he's talking about. Annie bites on

her hand to keep from laughing, like she can't be-lieeeeve we're getting to hear this. I bite on my hand too because I think I'm going to throw up. My eyes feel hot. I want us to get out of here.

"I found something spilled all over the inside of my briefcase when I went in it this morning. It's never happened before so I knew it had to be her. I think she may have thought I had money in there and gone in to get it."

Annie looks at me, puzzled. My heart is beating so loud I'm afraid she'll hear it and know my half smile is the hardest face I've ever made.

"That's absurd," Aunt Sarah says. "Megan probably wanted to get some paper to draw on."

I wait with the breath in my mouth turning old and sour from fear. I'm begging silently that somehow they will just drop the discussion and Annie and I can leave now.

Ice tinkles from one of their glasses. A few raindrops fall. That could save me. Maybe now he'll say, "Jesus we're in for a storm," and they'll both run into the house.

I let my breath out slowly and cross my fingers behind my back so tightly they almost break each other. Uncle Michael sighs heavily like someone with really bad news. "I didn't tell you the whole story about why she's here because I was afraid you'd say no and I owe her uncle Sean. His family pretty much raised me when Ma got sick. Even after she came home from the hospital. Hell, I was over there more than at my own house."

There's a little murmur from Aunt Sarah as if she's nodding with recollections of stories told and retold about Uncle Michael in his younger days, hanging out at the O'Hagens', thick as brothers.

"Anyway, Stephanie's mother just walked out on her and her father. A total alkie. Ugly as it gets. Liam met her years ago over a couple of shots. Classic bar slut. Shirt down to here, always smashed. He knocked her up and, of course, being the good Catholic, married her. Think that daughter's going to be just like her. Bad news. Confronted her tonight when I got home about going into my briefcase. Didn't even deny it."

A drink tinkles again. My eyes are glued on my dirty bare feet. There are no big words that can shield me from Annie's stare. I'm stained and filthy and naked. A gray, pulsing mollusk without a shell.

I shift slightly, still keeping my eyes down. I'm so hot inside I think my blood is on fire. There is no position I can move to, no place I can look to take away the even hotter blaze from Annie's eyes.

I try to swallow but my tongue is twice its normal size. I look into my stomach like I have x-ray vision. My guts are all moving aside to make room for the thick, hissing rattlers who ate all my words. The words that let me pretend I'm better than I really am. Because I really am just like my mother, right? A bar slut in the making. A bad seed getting ready to sprout.

I make another sick half smile. I wonder if I should impress Annie with what I really know. Tell her about my perfect memory for all the mixed drinks my mother makes when she talks about her great days in bartending. The perfect Rob Roy where you have to pour exactly a half ounce each of sweet and dry vermouth. The whiskey sour that is so much better with the mix from the yellow package than the brand with a girl in blue on the front. Maybe I can amaze Annie and all her rich friends with my ability to tell the difference between cheap scotch and twelve-year-old single malt just by the smell.

More rain falls on me. The chili dog I ate at the mall heaves in my stomach.

"Let's go before we're soaked," Annie says, and I see a slice of her face right before I turn around. Bright blue eyes opened wide, perfect eyebrows arching with just the faintest glimmer of superiority.

• • •

I'm numb during dinner. There's a funeral for Nancy Drew in my head. I've been stupid, a little kid holding on to fairy tales. Now I envision the beautiful sleuth murdering her famous lawyer father before turning the gun on herself. Hanna Gruen weeps openly beside the double caskets. Nancy's school chums look stupefied. Ned Nickerson ties and unties the arms of his college sweater over his shoulders, thinking he should have put his hand in Nancy's pants when he had the chance.

It's too late. We both need to move on.

I keep my face on my plate. It's some kind of stuffed noodles that everyone at the table calls *pasta,* like they're so cool and they know Italian or something. Uncle Michael is telling some stupid-ass story about some client he has who's opening a boys' school for troubled teens. Big deal. What does Uncle Michael expect, a medal for knowing him?

I watch Annie's brothers and they are all pigs slurping at their food. Funny how tonight Annie doesn't nudge my arm to see if I'm as sickened by their behavior as she is. I pick my eyes off of my plate and steal a look at Uncle Michael and Aunt Sarah. Maybe I should tell them that their precious daughter is into major hook-ups. Maybe I should tell them they're all a bunch of phonies and maybe they don't know how good it felt when my mother brushed my hair at night and told me what it would be like for us in the White House.

I don't even know if they're going to keep me here, and I hope they send me back to Boston so I can kick my father in the ass and tell him thanks a lot for the cell phone that he never sent me, which I could have at least used in private. He hasn't called me back since he left me that pathetic "Hey, kiddo" message.

Maybe my father hasn't called back because he only sees bar slut number two when he thinks about me. I'm not glamorous like my mother is, but I have her skin and her eyes, and some people say she looked like me when she was my age. I'm sure my dad hoped that I'd never be born. My upcoming existence took away his freedom. Maybe that's all I am to him, a reminder of the biggest mistake of his life. The reason he had to get married and ruin whatever rosy future he saw for himself.

Annie says, "Let's get out of here" right after dinner, but her face is hard when she looks at me, like having me go anywhere with her is the last thing she wants. As we walk toward the door, it takes everything I have not to rip out Megan's throat when Aunt Sarah kisses her softly on the head and tells her to pick out her favorite book.

We get on our bikes and start to pedal up the long path to our spot on Mulholland. I'm thinking I could ride into Annie when a car gets close so the family could scream at her funeral how they knew I was a bad seed and how they wished to dear God they had acted to evict me sooner.

I'm sweating slightly when we get to our spot even though it's cool enough for Annie to be wearing her new blue jacket, which makes her eyes look bright enough to light candles. Andrew's there and says, "Hi, Senator" the second I get off my bike.

I glance quickly at Annie to see if she's going to expose me. Her eyes lock onto mine and I brace myself for her announcement that I know the Kennedys like she knows the pope. She sweeps her eyes right past me and it hits me that it wouldn't exactly help her image if everyone knew her cousin's mother was a bar slut and a total alkie. Guess she's not too happy she told people we were cousins now.

I give a harsh laugh like I'm a biker chick challenged to a fight and swipe the back of my hand across my nose. I almost wish she would make her little announcement so that the crowd could rise against me and I could lash out with fists and nails, fighting until they stomped the last breath out of me, a martyr for all offspring of total alkie moms.

We walk up to the center of the circle. There are two brown bags. Andrew seems to be responsible for them and his dark eyes flash with rebellious excitement.

JKIII is nowhere to be seen and Annie is royally pissed. She takes out a cigarette and hands one to Leslie, Emily and Eva, letting me fend for myself. I see in the slight turn of her mouth that bringing me along is almost more than she can bear. That she now will begin to slowly and subtly wash her hands of me.

Ben walks up and Leslie flashes him a thousand-watt smile, sending off her own force field of hormones.

Matt says something to Andrew I can't hear. Andrew opens up one of the paper bags and pulls out a twelve-pack of beer. Everyone stops what they're doing and stares. Andrew looks proud of himself and says, "My mother's out of town. The new boyfriend. Nothing she'll notice. And besides, I'm celebrating. Feels so good to have the cast off." He holds up his newly emancipated arm, which is the pale brother of his suntanned one.

Like the junk food, it's different when rich people have alcohol and beer in their homes.

Andrew passes out beer to Matt, Brian, Ben and Carl. Annie and her girlfriends are studying their cigarettes like they've never watched the way they burn before. Andrew says, "Well, ladies?"

Everyone looks at Annie. I feel her on the fence, and in a flash I see her as the little Goody Two-shoes she was when she was Megan's age. I'm the bad seed, so I say, "I'm a little thirsty" in a cool voice, and everyone looks at me in surprise until Andrew says admiringly, "What do you expect from a senator from a big city?"

I take a beer, and then Eva and Annie hold out their hands for a beer at the same time. Leslie just giggles when Ben presses one into her hand. Emily's the last one without a beer and everyone just laughs when Andrew tosses one into her lap.

Bottle openers flip through the group. Emily's beer fizzes

over her hand. I've never seen beer that wasn't in cans and the smell of it almost makes me gag. It's her Saturday drink. What she has when she says she's not drinking because beer doesn't count.

Annie, back in the lead, takes the first sip. "Not bad," she says with a wise nod, then clinks her bottle with Eva's.

I take a sip. It's horrible. In my mouth, the smell that was her Saturday breath becomes the taste. Her angry fists are all around me. Silver bangles flash against the dark that is creeping down from the sky and making shadows of the other kids of raised bottles and open mouths.

I swallow my sip, then hold my breath while I take another and then another. My sips are getting bigger and bigger, turning into gulps that hit my throat like acid. In a moment I'm ready for another bottle and I flash my eyes at Annie, daring her to draw some genetic conclusion.

Andrew gets me another bottle and asks me if I want to go for a walk. Things are getting fuzzy, but I don't feel so angry anymore. Eva gives me a dirty look, but I only smile at her before saying, "Okay."

Andrew takes my hand. His fingers are strong and a lot bigger than mine. His sweatshirt is soft as it rubs on my bare shoulder, and I realize dimly that I'm cold and that I wish I had a cute little jacket to wear.

We walk for a while. The white rubber on the end of my old blue tennis shoes bats moonlight onto the path. Behind us, laughter rises in smug clouds of privilege and I know, twenty years from now, they'll all be lifting glasses at the club, dressed in clothes that cost what my dad makes in a year.

We get farther down the path, which has become narrower with the trees closing over us so that a couple of times I have to duck so I don't hit my head. I can barely see and I stumble. Andrew puts his arm around my shoulders to steady me, then keeps it there and says, "You're cold."

Out of the fuzziness I feel a whoosh of gratitude for his concern. We drink as we walk. He finishes his second bottle and motions to me to drink mine down. I hold the hard glass against my lips and let the beer slide down my throat. I almost can't even taste her now or remember the Saturday afternoons of slurred shouts and the time she knocked my head into the TV and tiny bits of glass burrowed into my hair while blood ran in rivers.

I hold my empty bottle up to his. He clinks it like a toast and I start laughing because it's so funny to clink something when it's empty. He laughs too and clinks my empty bottle again. That makes me laugh so hard that tears fall onto my cheeks.

He stops laughing and says, "Want to sit down?" I fall against him, wondering why my face is so wet.

He catches me and lowers us to the ground. We're lying on leaves that must be from last summer since they're dry and crackling. I want to ask what's up with his mom, the boyfriend and his dad, but he suddenly puts his lips against mine. I feel a full charge erupt through my body and I wonder if I have a mini force field of hormones that I'm giving off.

He keeps pressing his lips on mine and it's a way different feeling than I had kissing Carl last night in Bump Around. His lips feel like something crucial for my survival, like a secret antidote to a poison someone slipped into my meal. I like them pressing on mine. I like his smell of pure guy.

His hands stroke my shoulders and he kisses me on the lips in steady little tiny kisses that remind me of a woodpecker, so I start laughing so hard, I hiccup.

He laughs a little too, and then he pulls on my shirt, taking it out of my shorts, and puts his hand on my bare stomach. My skin vibrates like a chick out of its shell, with the air ruffling its tiny yellow feathers.

He pulls my face close to his. His eyes are closed so I close mine. I like this with just our foreheads touching. My brain had started to feel dizzy, but now he's steadying me. He isn't even kissing me anymore and I wonder if we're just going to stay with our heads touching for a while. It feels good, like we're letting our thoughts float into each other's heads. It feels safe and I wish we could do this forever.

Suddenly, he presses his lips up against mine and shoves his tongue into my mouth. I'm so shocked I almost gag but jerk my head back to force his tongue out. He must think I'm playing a game or something, because he puts his hands on the back of my head and sticks his drool-covered tongue back in even harder. I can't breathe. I'm gagging. The alcohol swims inside me.

My stomach heaves, like the little warning before a big earthquake, then an eruption of vomit rushes out, striking him in the face and practically hurling itself down his throat. He flings himself back like a wounded animal, howling in utter horror.

I throw up again, this time on the ground, and I see my shadow, pitching forward, emptying itself, just like I've seen her do, too many times to count.

I stumble to my feet. Is Andrew still around?

I look, squinting against the darkness between the trees,

struggling to see. He's nowhere. I vaguely remember him running off and calling me a bunch of names I could barely hear as I heaved. I have no idea how to get back to the group. Even though I got the alcohol out of my stomach, it still must be in my head, because I feel thick and stupid. There's moonlight, but many of the trees look the same and I'm not sure which way to go. I listen, hearing all the sounds of the woods, wishing I could transform myself into an animal and run for cover in the rustling leaves.

I turn in a full circle, smelling the vomit that must now be crusting on my clothes, seeing nothing familiar. I've never felt so alone in my life.

I walk a few random steps, then turn uncertainly and walk back the way I came. I do this several times, now with panic beating in my heart. What if I'm stuck here forever? What if I'm lying over a fallen log a month from now, starving and half dead, and a serial killer comes along?

"Hey!" I shout as loud as I can. My face is red in the night from shame, but my fear of being stuck here alone is even greater. Tears start running down my cheeks. "Hey, Annie. You guys!"

I hear shouts of male voices sparking on my right and I plunge ahead that way wildly, wishing I'd thought to grab a branch since I might run into coyotes along the way, waiting to devour me.

When I stumble into the clearing with a tear-stained face and smelling like vomit, all the voices melt away. The group, all relaxing around the flashlight bonfire, looks up at me and stares. No one stands up quickly to see if I'm okay. No one moves except for Matt, who sits up straight and says in a pretend principal's voice, "Um, if you're looking for Andrew, he went home. Apparently, there was some kind of an accident." Everyone totally cracks up. Annie laughs the hardest.

I walk over to my bike in silence, then slip my leg over the bar that's too high for me, wondering how or when I'm ever going to get off of their sterling silver planet.

CHAPTER ELEVEN

Annie says a frigid "Good night" to me when we walk into her house as if I'm some great weight she has to bear, and only because of her extraordinary breeding is she even doing me the favor of acknowledging my existence. I go straight into the bathroom in my room and crumple to the floor. While on my back, I peel off my clothes. Then I stand up and stumble into the shower. The water is warm and soothing on my body. I only wish that it could wash away everything that happened from the moment I thought about sneaking into that briefcase.

I scrub harder and harder, pouring gobs of shampoo onto

my hair and all over my body. Maybe if I wash hard enough, I can get down to the layers inside me that are my mom.

I flip the handle to cold and stand for a full minute as if it's a punishment I deserve. I towel off, then slide into a big white fluffy robe that, yes, is another thing the Sullivans have provided me. I walk into my bedroom and collapse on the bed. My fingers punch out my dad's cell phone.

He answers with a tired and defeated "Hello."

"Dad."

"Stephanie."

I try to hold back the tears. This is the only number I have to call and he is supposed to want me, but I can tell in that one word that he doesn't.

Too bad. He has to take me back. I've been here for four days, and now the thought of still being stuck here for school starts ticking like a terrifying explosive in the back of my brain. He's had enough time to, as Michael Sullivan said, clean up his mess.

"Dad, I need to come home."

"Yeah, yeah, kiddo, I miss you too. It's just that I'm still working on things here. Just for a little while longer."

His passivity only fuels my rage as if there's an ultimate

balance in the universe and the more still he is, the more whirling I become. "Dad," I say firmly, my voice another notch louder and higher.

"I know, I know. It's probably going to be just a few more days. I'll call you, okay?"

I can almost see his furtive hand pulling the phone away from his ear for a quick hangup. A quick getaway.

"No, it's not okay," I yell, pulling the phone back to his ear. "I need to come home now. NOW. Nothing is okay here. NOTHING. I have to get back and get ready for school. For once in your life, you HAVE TO DO SOMETHING."

I know my words slap him. I don't care. Fury is blasting off of me in unstoppable waves.

He doesn't say anything. Despair floats down, smothering my anger. I know he must now simply be standing stock still, like he always does when he just can't deal. I drop my voice. I can always beg. "Come on, Dad. Just call the airline and book my flight. Come on, please. I'll be fine at home. I'll stay out of your way—"

My tone moves him into action, but not the kind I wanted. "It just can't happen yet," he snaps and his tone is assertive for the first time, but only in preserving his defeat. "I'll call you in a couple of days," he says. He clicks off, not even risking a good-bye, just in case I have the audacity to continue to demand something more of him.

I lie on my bed staring at the ceiling. This is the part about my family nobody understands. My dad's not the long-suffering hero all his brothers think he is. He's not the real parent just because he's not the obvious, crazy drunk one. He is only a vague brush of air in my life, never anything I can actually hang on to.

When he's home, he's either reading his law books or grimly cleaning up one of my mom's messes. His interactions with me are nothing but a series of martyred sighs, strung together in one long exhale of defeat.

I caught him once staring at me when he thought I was asleep. I saw him, through the slits in my lashes, looking at me like I was the hangman's noose itself. Because, after all, if it wasn't for me happening, he and the bar slut would have simply parted ways.

At least, strange as it sounds, I know my mom really loved me. Yeah, she was drunk a lot and she hurt me. But when she was there, she was THERE. She pulsed with life. She gave me fantasies of us in the White House. She hugged me fiercely.

I clutch the robe around me and my mind floats to last summer. My mom took me on a picnic. She wasn't drinking. She had a little CD player with music from *The King and I*, our favorite musical. She taught me how to dance. Over and over she held my hands and sang, "Shall we dance, da, da, da, da, shall we dance," until we collapsed, laughing, onto the grass. Then we ate junk food until our stomachs were stuffed. At the end of the day she stroked my hair and whispered, "You're the most important thing in my life. No matter what ever happens, never forget that."

I wonder where she is now. I wonder if I'm still important to her.

• • •

I sleep late, awakened by an undercurrent I can feel more than hear. I slide out of bed, throw on shorts and a shirt, then slip into the hall. Voices rise from the patio: Annie's, sharp with anger, and her mother's, mollifying.

Since I can't hide up in my room all day and I don't have a plane ticket out of here, I figure I might as well go downstairs and face whatever's up.

I make a lot of noise as I walk into the kitchen. If they're talking about me, I don't want to hear it. The chatting I overheard under the gazebo last night was enough overheard conversation for a lifetime.

I say a loud good morning to Carmen. The chatter outside abruptly stops. I feel the tug in my stomach. It's not always great to be right. Obviously, they *were* talking about me. And I can guess: Annie's probably telling her mother it isn't fair that she's stuck with me; her mom is probably telling her that it's not for that much longer and she should be nice to people who are less fortunate than she is.

Great. Now it's all out in the open. I'm officially Annie's social charity case.

Aunt Sarah comes into the kitchen and gives me a fake smile so big you could drive a truck through it. "Good morning, Stephanie. I'm driving up to the club for my lesson today, if you girls want a ride."

"We have our bikes," Annie glowers.

"Well, okay," Aunt Happy continues. "But, if you change your mind . . . I'm leaving in half an hour."

Annie takes a blueberry yogurt out of the fridge and heads for the stairs. "I'll meet you in the garage in ten minutes," she barks at me. "If you're coming."

I give a small, little shrug that she doesn't even see because she's already turned her back to me. I'd like to just stay up in my room, but I know that Aunt Sarah is having lunch guests on the patio after her tennis lesson, and what if they wanted a tour of the house or something, and she opened my bedroom door to show them her beautiful taste in decorating, and there I was, huddled in the bed, like a hunchback in the attic?

I eat half a bagel really fast and run upstairs to get my bathing suit. Right before I leave my room, I turn around toward the bookshelf. I need the comfort of words, but Nancy Drew is dead to me now. I skim the titles, then grab a biography on Harriet Tubman. We covered her in school. She was a brave woman who risked her life to free slaves. I'm only going to read about real people now. Real people who did real things. No more fairy tales. I meet Annie in the garage for a long and silent ride to the club.

When we get to the deck at the club it's sunny and really hot. Emily, Leslie and Eva are in lounge chairs today instead of in a close nest of towels just on the deck. The chair between Leslie and Eva is open, reserved for the queen. Annie walks right to it and drops down her towel. There's a chair open on the end next to Emily. I put down my stuff there.

There's a pounding on the stairs and JKIII, Matt, Brian,

Ben and Carl run up, soaking from the pool, and shake water all over Leslie and Annie, who fake-scream. I see Andrew behind them and my mouth dries. I turn to Emily and say, "Do you need some lotion?" to try to be engaged in conversation and not expected to look at him. She's bent in toward the other girls and doesn't even respond.

None of the girls have said anything to me about throwing up all over Andrew last night, including Annie, but apparently the guy world is something different. It appears that it's all they've been talking about all morning, judging from the reenactment that Matt and Brian are engaged in where Matt is saying, "Oh, Andrew, you're so hot, you're so hot, you're so *agggghhhhh.*" And he does a mock hurl on Brian.

Everyone laughs long and hard. All the girls included, except, of course, me.

I feel even sicker than I did last night. I know other kids must throw up when they drink and it's probably something that would go away if I just could be like Annie and make some sort of flirtatious joke out of it. But I have no idea how to do that and I can see that Andrew doesn't either. I've embarrassed him in the eyes of his friends and I'm sure he'll never forgive me. He can't even look at me.

I lie against the back of my seat and just close my eyes. I

never even realized how good I had it at my old school when I was just invisible. I had always thought that being ignored was the bottom of the social pyramid because you didn't really exist to anyone. Now I know there's something even worse. Being visible and then disgraced. Once you're disgraced, you can never just be invisible. The second people see you, they remember The Story. You feel the hot flames of shame, over and over, with every knowing glance and every whisper.

I open my eyes for a minute and grab my backpack. I root around for the Tubman bio. The tension in my body starts to ease as I devour the story about a strong-minded runaway slave who led hundreds of slaves to freedom along the Underground Railroad.

Amal, the bombshell, and her red-haired friend walk up the deck. The guys are playing Nerf football but I can tell they've spotted them. I sneak a glance at Annie. She puts a huge smile over her blinding teeth and walks right toward them.

"Hey," she calls out when she's halfway there. "Are you guys new here? Do you want to come over and join us?"

I can't see Amal's face, but she and the redhead sort of shrug, then walk toward us. I think Annie must have gone insane until I catch Eva's expression. Her eyebrows are slightly raised in a half-mocking yet congratulatory arch. I suddenly get it. Annie is a general making friends with the enemy before the enemy knows she's the enemy. Very, very smart.

Amal stands over us with her towel. Annie has us all move our chairs back so we can make room for Amal and her friend's chairs. Annie watches over the movement like she's invited over an empress from another land, and then she makes the introductions. Leslie, as usual, says "Hi" in a funny voice. Emily looks sleepy, and Eva sharp and brittle, waiting to see if the new person will make her social position with Annie more or less stable. Will Annie need her old lieutenant to strategize with, or will the newcomer totally replace any need for Eva at all?

When Annie gets to me, she says, "This is Stephanie. She's from Boston and visiting my family for a little while. Her uncle was really good friends with my dad when they were growing up, so when she first got here, we pretended we were cousins, just for fun."

Her words hit me like knives. She's done it now, she's severed my lifeline. I'm not part of her family so no one in her group has to include me anymore. Emily and Leslie delicately turn their heads from me as if it'd be in poor taste to see raw humiliation so up close and personal.

Eva glows. She turns to me with a smile of the deepest satisfaction. "I knew it," she says, loud enough for everyone to hear. "I mean, look at them. Hel-lo. I mean, could any two people be more different?"

They all pause to run their eyes worshipfully over Annie, then cruelly over me. Our contrast is brutal. The bright and the dark. The treasure and the trash. Now that Annie has deftly woven in this bit of information that frees her from any blood connection with me, it's just a matter of time before she lets it all come out. What she's had to *deal* with for these long days. The burden of being stuck with the pathetic offspring of a total alkie.

I get smaller and smaller on the sundeck as Annie bustles further in her role as social director, getting more and more information out of the newcomers. The redhead's name is Kathy. She's actually a member of the club, but she never comes and she goes to a different school than Annie and her friends so they've never met. She was friends with the bombshell in Georgia before she moved here three years ago. Their dads worked together. Both the bombshell and her friend talk totally southern. Their accents are the last nail in my coffin. The one chip I had to maybe get back in this group was my accent. Now my uniqueness is gone.

Someone throws the Nerf football off the deck and the guys amble over like sweaty warriors. Annie's eyes are extra bright when she introduces JKIII to Amal as if she's just waiting for JKIII's face to show interest. He only acts polite and Annie tosses her hair wildly up into the sun as if she's a horse on the open range, head of the herd, with no competitors.

Annie does more introductions. While everyone's saying "hi-nice-to-meet-you," I have a chance to study the southern goddess. Her black hair is heavy and wavy like my mother's and like mine. Her eyes are black and enormous, but not like a woman's, more like a little girl who has a secret Raggedy Ann at home in her closet she still hugs when nobody is looking.

Her face doesn't match her body, which is so grown up, all the boys seem almost afraid of her.

When she speaks she seems even younger than fourteen, as if she's unsure of herself and shy. Annie's asking her questions about where she came from and why she moved here. She says her dad used to teach chemistry at some university in Georgia but came here for business.

The more questions Annie asks, the more Amal seems to

shrink and Annie to grow. Annie acts interested in hearing her story, but her questions are really needles that prick the bombshell's face to show her quiet, stumbling nature and her unease with the spotlight.

Annie closes by saying, "You're going to have a great time here," and doesn't even lose one ounce of her aggressively shimmering light when the bombshell takes off her sundress to reveal anew her amazing landscape of curves and valleys.

• • •

It's after six. Clouds streak the deepening blue sky and a hint of cool bites the air. An adult looking at us on the sundeck would just think the scene was of some kids lying out in the sun, but really, so much has happened in the last couple of hours. Annie has waged a formidable covert battle and won. She has taken a girl who is prettier than she is and made her beholden to her. Annie has demonstrated that she is keeper of the keys, and that all things included in this ready-made group of fabulous friends come only through her largesse.

Amal now automatically looks to Annie when any decisions need to be made. The queen has added her latest subject.

We're packing up our stuff and everyone's going to Annie's to get something to eat and play pool. Her parents are going to the Hollywood Bowl tonight and Annie's already texted their housekeeper, who, of course, also has a BlackBerry, to tell her that people are coming over for a party and to make sure Megan's out of the way. Her brothers left yesterday for school so Annie will have full reign of her house.

We glide down the hill from the club. Matt and Brian race each other. JKIII rides by Annie, grabbing her butt. The goddess is on Annie's left. Kathy, her attendant, rides next to her as if to protect her full figure from any grasping wind. Kathy is starting school tomorrow. Annie and her friends still have a couple more days.

My dad better get me out of here before then.

We pour into Annie's house. Carmen, as instructed, is upstairs playing some baby game with Megan. Annie throws chips into bowls and tells me to get sodas. We go into the billiard room and Annie says, "Hey, Amal, you want to break?" like she's known people named "Amal" her whole life.

Amal giggles and says she's never played before and that she'll just watch. Annie says, "No watching allowed, you can be with me." She gives Amal a pool cue, tosses one to JKIII and says to him, with a last kicking of dust on my grave, "Tell Andrew he's your partner."

• • •

The game goes on for forever. Amal has a baby voice on top of her southern accent, which everyone just seems to find so charming.

In normal times, I'd consider eating chips to help promote my boob growth, but I'm never going to have any friends or boyfriends again anyway, so what's the point?

Amal is terrible at pool but no one playing seems to care. Annie's become her big sister. Andrew has become the Big Demonstrator. Twice, he's stood behind her and put the cue in her hands to line up her shot.

I float through the party, a stranger from a strange planet, passing little knots of conversations that are impossible to join.

Their pool game ends just as the doorbell rings for the pizza guy. Annie screams she's coming. The guys follow her to the door to carry the boxes of pizza into the kitchen. Annie tells me to get the paper plates.

I don't really like being ordered around, but there's not much else you can do but try to help once you've been disgraced.

All the guys fold their pizza in half and shove it in their mouths. All the girls bite off tiny pieces and act like they're not that hungry even though I know they are. Everyone keeps asking Amal questions about Georgia and having her say words with her accent. It's too painful to watch.

I slip outside, planning to say I'm too hot if anyone asks, but nobody notices. I've been out there alone, sitting in the gazebo at the far end of the yard, for more than an hour when the rest of them tumble out to play night volleyball.

I can hear their shouts glide on the wind. Laughter rolls up in short duets, high for the girls, low for the guys. No one is wondering where I am. No concerned faces come and ask what's up with me.

Shadows of two of the girls leave the volleyball net and I make my way up behind them. Leslie and Emily sit on one of the stone benches taking a cigarette break. I'm silent as I approach. Leslie picks her hair up off her neck like she's a little sweaty from the game.

I'm just about to open up, take the risk and say, "What's up" or something, like maybe, even if I'm not Annie's cousin and even if I did barf all over Andrew last night, they'll at least think they can talk to me because I'm Annie's houseguest. I clear my throat and start to open my mouth when I hear Amal scream, "So this is what y'all do in California," and Andrew tackles her, making sure he lands beneath her, protecting her from the ground.

I swallow the words in a sawdust throat, then scuttle back into the shadows.

CHAPTER TWELVE

Amal's crush on Andrew scurries around our nest of towels like dry leaves before a tornado. It rises in the air to zing through the quick glances between Annie, Leslie and Emily, then finally rests in my neck muscles and forehead that feel as if they've been hit by a baseball bat.

Eva's not at the club yet and neither are any of the guys. I lie on my towel and close my eyes. Even though I slipped upstairs to bed a little while after Andrew's big tackle last night, I didn't sleep for hours. At first, it was just too noisy. Music blared and people shouted. Then later, when the music wasn't so loud, it was the quiet laughter that kept my eyes stuck open, high, golden notes of merriment that leapt into my room and fell over my body like a cage.

I slit my lids to see what's happening. Am I so far out of the group that there will be no official mourning for me? Will absolutely none of the flurry of feminine support that surrounded Annie when JKIII made his comment about Amal being hot come to my aid? Will there be no conversation at all about how I liked a boy, who seemed to like me, who now likes someone else?

Annie says the worst possible thing. "Where did you go off to last night? Carl was looking for you."

Ah, now my role is clear. None of them would ever like Carl, but if I'm stuck hanging around, maybe Annie can pawn me off on him. Maybe he will keep me out of her hair until the blessed time when her mother can shove my butt on a plane and get me out of her life. Outrage makes my tongue dry. How dare she toss Carl at me like a scrap from Amal's feasting on Andrew?

I pour some lotion on my stomach, concentrating on making a perfect circle. Neither Leslie nor Emily speak. Annie's word is law. There will be no rallying of support and outpouring of sympathy. I have slipped from my lofty perch as a cousin of the queen and slid into the vague role of peasant. I am now The Expendable One. Just like Carl is expendable in their guy world, carrying their stuff or picking up everyone's food at the club when their number is called.

In addition to my utter demotion, there exists the much more important issue of the new force in town. Nothing can interfere with the courting of Amal as Friend. Nothing can stop the crescendo of energy required to gather her into their midst, mark her with their words, phrases and private jokes so that they never have to fear her coming at them. Never have to turn a corner and see her stealing one of their own, one of their guys. The fact that she stole Andrew from me is of no consequence. I don't matter.

Carl comes up to us and sits by Emily. He says hi to all of us. Everyone says hi back to him, and when I do it, he blushes and Leslie nudges him in the arm and giggles. Annie gives me a sharp look and I force a half giggle. I feel as if I've just opened another box of faded hand-me-downs from my older cousins.

Emily and Leslie giggle again. My mouth is too stiff to go up into another giggle. I still feel a sharp needle in my heart when I think about Andrew. I really liked him, and then poof, like that, it's all over.

I need to turn over on my stomach, close my eyes and fade

into the world of Harriet Tubman, just to get my bearings. Since I've buried Nancy Drew I get headaches from having to be me for so long.

When I'm only on my side, just about to roll onto my stomach, slapping and pushing rumbles from the stairs and I know that the rest of the group is here. I hurry and fall onto my towel. I don't have time to unhook my strap and I hope nobody will know I'm faking concentrating on my tan because the girls never leave the straps across their backs.

The herd thunders toward us. There's a jostling around the towels. Amal's southern accent is being tried on by all the guys, especially Andrew. Annie and Amal lie next to each other and speak in excited whispers. I hear Annie say, "because both our names start with A," and they both laugh.

Sharp betrayal lances my stomach. I hate Annie for ousting me and bringing this enemy into our camp. I blame Annie for having Andrew get a crush on Amal.

But really, down deep, I blame myself. I blame myself for being my mother's daughter. I got drunk. I threw up. I disgraced myself.

Explosive laughter rises from one of the guys who picks up on the Amal-Annie thing. Matt says, "Their names both start with A, all right," like having a name start with A is the Jeopardy answer to, "Why are these two women both goddesses?"

JKIII asks who wants to go swimming. Annie and Amal say they'll go, and they laugh when they say it. I hear them clamor toward the steps. I keep my eyes closed.

Music filters up to my ears. Leslie's iPod is plugged into a dock. Some song is playing about a girl who gets dumped by a guy.

My mind flickers. This is my song. Mine after Andrew walks out on me and our three kids. I see myself standing in the doorway of a humble home with green shutters and a swing set in the backyard, crying, while Andrew walks into the rain and gets into a car driven by Amal and her big boobs.

I sink farther into my towel. Sweat pools in the center of my back. Tears sneak out of my eyes. I pull my T-shirt over my face so I'm in a tiny white tent with only room enough to breathe. I open my eyes. Light comes in but it's soft. Bad feelings rush into my stomach like they've been stuffed into my feet and have finally escaped. More and more tears pour out, and I wish another song would come on.

I do a new trick where I bite on my lip really hard so a little drop of blood comes into my mouth. I think of the pierce in my lip as being half of a snakebite. It almost helps push the bad stuff back into my feet, but then my mother's face comes roaring up. She's telling the doctor I broke my arm when I fell down the stairs, and I'm too afraid to tell him about the shiny silver bangles, the red flashing nails and her face squeezed in so much anger that I saw worms pour out of her eyes.

A new song comes on with a fast beat. It's too hot in my T-shirt tent, and I think my tears have turned to steam.

I hear the crack of chairs on deck and I can tell that Eva, Emily and Leslie are reconfiguring their chairs so that their heads will all be really close together. I'm on the chair right next to them but I'm now so irrelevant, they don't even care if I hear or not. I'm just like the guy flipping burgers at the snack bar, whom they never see, even when they're gossiping right in front of him.

Eva's whisper to the other girls cuts through the sounds of far-off splashing and laughing. "It's not like her body is that great. I mean, in five years, she'll be totally fat."

Dangerous ground, you'd think, to say to Leslie, considering that she is plump herself.

"Totally," Leslie tosses in. "I mean, I *know* I'm overweight, so I don't go parading myself around like she does. She doesn't even seem to think about it. Like she is just so sexy that no one even notices all her fat."

So, apparently, the subject of fat is always a safe arrow to sling, just as long as one acknowledges her own imperfections first.

I slip my shirt tent to the side and look at Amal emerging from the water. I hadn't gotten past the breasts before, but if I look hard enough, I guess I can see a little extra flesh at the thighs and a softness around her middle.

The three of them are just getting started. Emily, the sleepy peach, speaks in the most animated voice I have heard from her yet, as if nothing before has ever been as interesting as the dissection of Amal's fat.

"Annie said last night that when we were all walking out of the club, Amal took one of the cookies. You know, the ones that they always have out for the guests by the front door?" They all murmur ascent and even I know what they're talking about, because every day, Carl makes a trip to get a bunch of the free, giant chocolate chip cookies for the group. The guys all stuff a few in their mouths, but the girls only split one, between all of them, talking about sugar, carbs and fat grams even while they're eating it.

Emily goes on, "Well, Annie said that Amal scarfed a

whole cookie down, by herself. Then, she said to Annie, 'Aren't you getting one?' and Annie goes, 'What, with these thighs?' And Amal just goes, 'Well, they're really good.'"

Emily sniffs. "Amal never even said one thing in defense of Annie's thighs, or one thing bad about her own. Like she obviously really thinks she's like a supermodel."

They lean in even closer to each other. More venom spews from their lips. They go on to describe more and more ugly and repulsive aspects of Amal, all of which they have found out through Amal's supposed new best friend, Annie.

Down below, in the water, Amal shrieks with laughter as she and Annie run away from the boys together, not realizing how false her position in this whole group is, and that if she wasn't just so formidably beautiful, she would be cast adrift into the deep end, just like I am, with no one to save her from drowning.

CHAPTER THIRTEEN

The phone is slippery in my hand from sweat. My dad's voice is thin and jerky like a small woodland animal constantly on the run. I ask him again if I can come home NOW because I have to get ready to start high school in Boston. Where I belong. He doesn't answer. I can feel him scurrying for cover under an old log or pile of leaves. When he finally speaks, his voice is raspy, as if it's hard coming back from being an animal and having to turn back into a dad. "Not quite yet," he says. "But it won't be real long. Your mother and I are finally talking. Maybe about getting her into a rehab."

Talking? Rehab? What the hell does all that mean? I clear my throat and give in to the anger. "So, why can't you guys talk while I'm home?" I demand.

"It's not that simple," he says, running back through the woods. "The rehab is a live-in program. Minimum thirty days, but they like you to stay ninety."

Poison wells in my throat like I'm a human blowgun. Is he kidding? He's going to leave me stranded in the inner circle of hell for a minimum of thirty days? I open my mouth to release the darts defining his endless inadequacies when I suddenly stop. My mother's face shrieks into the airspace in front of me. Her face is contorted with contempt. Rage bulges under her cheekbones.

I stand up and look in the mirror. My mother's furious black eyes snap back at me. My breath draws in sharply. I take in my bunched cheeks and bitter sneer. Vignettes roll of so many moments watching my dad limp along after being lashed by her barbed tongue. I'm frozen in horror of who I've become. First the drinking and now this.

Am I going to start hitting next?

All my rage dissipates. "Whatever," I whisper.

My father tries a fake-robust laugh and says, "I've already

squared it with Michael and Sarah. Annie's school sounds amazing."

"Right," I spit dryly, unable to resist rearing her head for one last barb. "Amazing."

I sit at the edge of my bed and stare out the window for what seems like hours. There's a knock at my bedroom door before Aunt Sarah enters and hands me two uniforms that she says I'll be wearing to Annie's school. I didn't know they wore uniforms in schools that weren't Catholic. In the public school in my neighborhood, the kids all wear jeans and the girls wear short shirts that show off swatches of their stomachs even in winter. But then, Annie's school isn't public. It's rich-kid private.

Aunt Sarah sits on my bed and explains how Annie's school normally works. She says the kids have to fill out applications, take tests and have interviews. She tells me I won't have to do any of that because I'm there under special circumstances and that she doesn't want me worrying about tuition because she and Uncle Michael have it covered.

The word *tuition* falls out of her mouth and sits in a prickly lump between us. It's like when Uncle Michael reminded me that he was paying for my food and stuff. I wasn't even thinking that anyone would have to spend money for me to go to school because all kids have to go to school and I thought that was just what grown-ups made us do because it was the law. Now, I'm falling down a mountain with the porcupine of tuition clutching at my throat, sticking needles in my hands when I try to pull it off. Aunt Sarah wants me to know they're not just putting me up and buying me food; they are spending lots of money to educate me. And there's no doubt, she wishes she were done with me so she could just focus on her perfect family of popular, attractive kids.

I feel profoundly embarrassed, like I'm a kid on a milk carton that Aunt Sarah heroically rescued from a trash can, only to discover that the parents don't want it and now she's going to have to let something of a vague and dirty origin live inside her pristine home. Ever since she had the conversation with Uncle Michael in the gazebo, she watches me all the time, especially if Megan's around, as if I might try to slip alcohol into her milk or teach her drunken swear words.

I make a vow that I will repay Aunt Sarah and Uncle Michael every penny for my tuition and for all the food I've eaten here and the uniforms she's bought for me.

She keeps looking at me with eyes that take in everything from the scabs on my knuckles to my ragged fingernails. "Thanks so much for everything," I say, but I have to look down at my hands when I say this because I'm ashamed and sorry that she's stuck with me.

"Oh, that's okay, of course," she says, but it's really not okay and we both know it.

She closes the door behind her and I hold up the uniform and try to beat back the dread. We start tomorrow. Annie told me that Monday and Tuesday are only for orientation which is a total joke. She's planning a big sleepover on Monday night so that everyone can gossip about the first day. I already have nothing to say.

• • •

Annie ignores me and talks nonstop to Aunt Sarah while she drives us to school. She's excited that this year she and her friends will rule the school because they're finally the oldest.

I already spent a year being the oldest—in middle school. Not once did I feel as though I ruled anything.

I can tell that she and Aunt Sarah had another fight when she found out I was starting school with her. I don't think she ever imagined I'd still be hanging around when her precious school started. When I walked out onto the patio last night, she and her mom abruptly stopped talking and then she asked me some fake question about whether I was ready for the big day.

I feel sick to my stomach. I don't want to go to this school with uniforms that are an expensive soft wool and not plaid at all like at Catholic school, but maroon with white shirts trimmed in maroon piping. I won't have a library to hide in here and a Father Patrick who knows I just want to read and be left alone. I'm going to have to sit with other kids in the cafeteria. Kids who act like they like you to your face and then talk about your fat behind your back.

Aunt Sarah pulls up a winding road off of Mulholland. A sign in white letters on a black background says CHAPMAN ACADEMY. She and Annie keep referring to the "campus." I don't even know what that is, but as Aunt Sarah pulls up, I see four different buildings with athletic fields, tennis courts, and an actual stable and horse ring.

I feel a surge of panic like a waterfall of acid in my stomach. Annie's dutifully telling me who I have for chemistry and algebra, but her voice comes at me in muffled clouds. I have a piece of paper with my schedule on it in my hand. It's already soft, like a baby's blanket, because I've been rubbing it together so much. I want to beg Annie not to leave me, at least not for the first day, but I know if I did, her eyes would become hard and she'd look at me like I was a bug with thick, hairy legs.

"Okay, girls," Aunt Sarah says. "Have fun." She pulls her car to the curb. Annie jumps out, not even waiting for me as she pours into the sea of students, all knowing exactly where they're going.

I hurry to keep up with Annie, whose uniform is hemmed as short as the school regulations allow. She walks quickly, tall and erect, fully aware that the flash of her blond hair and movement of her hips earn her glances from both girls and guys. She walks straight for the building closest to the tennis courts. It's brick, covered with ivy, like a college building in a movie. There's a bunch of guys hanging out on the steps. She slows to let me catch up and I know it's only because she needs to be able to pretend she's engrossed in conversation so she can pretend to ignore them.

"We have Specter for algebra," she whispers to me, but her eyes stay on the guys. "He's, like, so lost."

I nod, holding down pure terror as I mount the stairs next to her.

• • •

Our first class, social studies, has fifteen kids. Mr. Baker has two assistants, one young woman with short, blond, fake-messy hair, who knows a lot of the kids from last year and gives out a lot of fist bumps, and another woman who's older and wears metal glasses that are too skinny for her face and couldn't give a fist bump if her life depended on it.

We don't get any work today. Mr. Baker tells us to get "acclimated." I think how the nuns would scorn him with his wasted workday and his hip, spiky hair, how they would see right through to his desperate clinging to youth, with his tailored shirt that shows off his muscles but also forces his gut to strain against the fabric.

All seats are assigned by the alphabet. I'm on the opposite side of the room from Annie. I look around at the kids sitting next to me, but they just glide their eyes over me, looking to make eye contact with someone important.

Mr. Baker has passed out what he calls our "syllabus." We're supposed to be reading it. I can tell that Annie isn't, because she's whispering and giggling. I keep my eyes glued to it, but then all the noise is sucked out of the room and

I look up to see Amal the bombshell, who just walked in late.

In Catholic school she would have been in so much trouble, even on the first day. Mr. Baker acts like she's the guest of honor at his tea party. He personally escorts her to her seat. The other kids all watch her and I notice with horror that Andrew is also in my class, sitting in the far back of my row.

Annie waves to Amal and gives her a huge "Hey," but I can see, even from where I sit, that Annie didn't really want such a burning comet in her private Milky Way.

We have the same section, with the same kids, for all our classes. That means I'll see Annie, Andrew and Amal all day long. I'm beginning to hate the letter A. I don't know which section Emily, Leslie and the other guys are in; there are three sections in each grade.

I look down at the syllabus but I can't read a word. Whispers and giggles punch me. I think all the kids must be looking at me. Their laughter sounds cruel, as if they can see how lonely I am and it only makes me more ridiculous. I turn around to look at the clock in the back of the room and I see Andrew shoot a tiny plane at Amal.

Mr. Baker claps his hands together to get our attention and then tells us what he's going to expect from us this year. His words are muffled and they come at me from a million miles away. It's hard to breathe in here and I feel as if I might suffocate. There's a pounding in my head and I know it must echo the heartbeats of Amal and Andrew that pulse with excitement, desperate for the time when they can be alone together.

• • •

Annie walks down the hall with the strong steps of ownership, with Amal right beside her. I'm right behind them, because Annie said, "Come on" to me in an irritated voice as we walked out of class because I'm sure Aunt Sarah told her she has to help me the first day. They stop in the middle of the hall when two really cute guys wave and walk toward them. Right before the guys get to them, Annie clutches Amal's arm and whispers, "They go away every summer. They're cousins. Only in our grade, but totally gorgeous."

I'm sure Amal can see that for herself. They both have wavy brown hair, blue eyes and strong-jawed, summer-on-the-sailboat tans. The one on the left says, "Hey," and they both stop. I've caught up with Annie and Amal by now. Annie stands in the middle with Amal and me on either side.

Both guys stare at Amal. "New?" the one who said "hey" asks.

Amal blushes and looks down. "Just moved," Annie reports. "Bet you wish you stayed here for the summer," she adds, making herself unthreatened by Amal's beauty by becoming an amused commentator.

"I'm Gary," the one who hasn't said anything yet says.

"And this is Chandler," Annie adds, not wanting to slip out of focus during any introductions.

Amal picks her eyes up, but keeps her head down a little. "I'm Amal," she says.

"She's from Georgia," Annie fills in.

"I didn't know Amal was a southern name," Gary says.

Amal's head lifts just a little. "It's actually Arabic." She looks down, embarrassed.

Both Gary and Chandler are enormously charmed. Chandler steps a little closer to her and makes his voice come out in sort of a fake whisper. "So, tell me the truth, are you really an Arabian princess?"

"She's—" Annie starts to offer but Amal cuts her off. "Not

even close" comes out in a voice so soft the guys almost have to lean forward to hear.

Gary and Chandler laugh as if this is the funniest thing they've ever heard. Annie has two high spots of color on her cheeks. "Let's go," she says brusquely.

"Wait," Gary says, clearly wanting to prolong the moment. "Who's this?" and he jerks his head at me.

"She's not here for very long. My parents just have to take care of her for a while," Annie says impatiently and starts to plow forward. "Come on, we're going to be late for class."

Amal hurries with her. I stumble after them, willing the tears not to fall.

• • •

The English teacher's name is Mrs. Applebaum, but she tells us to call her "Wendy." At first I hate her. She's too informal-California like the rest of this horrible city. I miss the nuns who don't accept nonsense. "Wendy" passes out her syllabus. At first, I don't even read it because I'm scorning her and everything she stands for. Then I look down and I see the names of the writers sprinkled down the pages like an assembly sent to meet me at the airport, all bearing the smiles of

Auntie Em and Uncle Henry when Dorothy wakes up. My tears almost tumble down now, not from loneliness but from happiness. I have read every book on this list. There may be a refuge for me after all.

• • •

I've found the library and I slip in knowing I can avoid the cafeteria. Aunt Sarah gave me money for lunch, but I'd rather eat nothing than have to deal with where to sit and all that. I'm just settling in at a table, ready to browse the soothing shelves, when Annie comes up and tells me that I have to leave. She tells a couple of other random kids that too, and she sparkles and surges as if she's throwing a party. She pushes me and the other kids out the door, whispering, "It's kind of private."

I sneak a look around her and see Amal in the far corner of the library by the window. She's on her knees, bowing. Annie says she does this five times a day and that Mr. Campbell, who is really cute and the school counselor, has designated this corner as hers for her noon prayer.

Gary and Chandler, who've obviously been looking for Amal, try to push past Annie in a pretend football move and she half squeals and says, "Am I going to have to call the principal on you two?" She laughs when she says this and her hormone force field zings around all three of them in blinding spurts of stars.

I stand at the drinking fountain and bend toward the water because it's a place where you can hide in the middle of a crowd. A minute later, Amal comes out followed by Andrew, whom Annie allowed to stay in the library during Amal's bows. Gary and Chandler look quickly at Amal, then at Andrew, like they're not sure if something is going on or not. Chandler says, "Princess, may I escort you to the cafeteria?" and holds out his arm.

Andrew's eyes flash in black fury, but he just smiles and says, "Don't think so, bro," then edges himself between Chandler and Amal and walks her down the hall without seeing me, even when he passes within two inches of my face.

CHAPTER FOURTEEN

Annie is furious at her mother because she forgot to turn off the sprinkler system in the afternoon, in honor of her upcoming sleepover, and the grass is soaking wet, so we have to sleep in the family room instead of the tent. Aunt Sarah keeps saying, "I know you're upset" while Annie rants and raves. "How *could* you do this to me when you *knew* I was going to have a sleepover? We *always* sleep outside."

I'm sitting at the kitchen table acting like I'm reviewing the syllabus for English class, but really I'm studying Annie. Her nostrils flare sharply when she says for the third time how it's typical that no one ever thinks of her, ever. She brings up some birthday slight of a few years ago, where she told her mother at least ten times she wanted cream cheese frosting and she got chocolate. Her sense of being a victim energizes her. She puts her face closer and closer to Aunt Sarah's and says she's surprised her birthday is ever remembered at all.

I've seen the bounty of her closets and her jewelry box. I have to turn away. I focus on Aunt Sarah, who walks over to the oven to put in some giant pretzels that she's baking for the sleepover. She looks hazy and undefined as if she's a giant sponge, absorbing all the insults her daughter throws at her into the soft flesh around her chin and upper arms.

In the dim light of the afternoon, I see Aunt Sarah without the small lines around her eyes and mouth. I see her in high school, plain but wanting to fit in with the cool kids, dressed in expensive clothes, hovering near a queen like her daughter, maybe playing the mom like Leslie does or the quiet, unthreatening confidant like Emily. It must be because she marvels at the stunning physical beauty of her daughter, and feels some vague possessive interest in it, that she puts up with the onslaught of poison that spews from her child's mouth and covers the kitchen in a diaphanous orange glaze.

Leslie and Emily arrive first. They're giggly and filled with "omigods" when they hear we have to sleep indoors. Eva comes next, and she and Annie huddle together, making cracks about Amal's baby voice.

When Amal rings the bell, Annie runs to let her in and hugs her as if she's a best friend she hasn't seen in five years. I see Annie's profile during the hug, since she's on the side of Amal's head and Amal can't see her. For a second, Annie drops the fake smile. So far, her plan is working perfectly: she's conquered her enemy and neutralized the threat of Amal's allure to anyone male by digging in her claim for Amal's loyalty.

"We have to sleep in the family room," Annie says disgustedly. "My mother forgot to turn off the sprinklers."

Amal just shrugs and looks around shyly. Separated from the ferocious gregariousness of Annie, her eyes look wide and nervous, like a little girl's at someone's house she doesn't know well. I don't like to see her face without her body because then I feel guilty for hating her, as if I'm just hating some innocent kid who had nothing to do with stealing the boy I wanted to be my boyfriend.

I see Eva and Annie exchange eye contact when Amal unconsciously grabs a handful of chips. None of the other girls would ever eat chips at the beginning of a party if they didn't know any of the other girls that well, and didn't know if everyone else was going to eat chips that night or if boys were coming over.

Annie's and my sleeping bags are already spread out next to each other, starting a circle on the thick rug covering the dark wood of the family room. Leslie puts hers on the other side of Annie, and Emily puts hers next to Leslie's. Amal and Eva walk in with their bags at the same time. Annie takes Amal's out of her hands and walks over to where mine is. She kicks mine over and puts Amal's right next to hers. "Stephie won't mind," she says.

I'm so embarrassed I can't even look up. I just watch Eva's legs as she puts hers on the other side of Amal's, further shoving mine to the side.

The guy with gourmet Chinese food comes and Annie runs to get it. I ignore her in case she thinks she's going to ask me to get the paper plates. She brings the food to the center point where all the sleeping bags meet. The other girls go and sit on their bags. Amal smiles at me when I finally walk over to mine. I don't even bother to smile back.

Amal's eyes flash me a quick look of hurt, like a well-loved family dog that's suddenly kicked in the face. I'm furious with her for trying to make me feel bad when she's the one who walked into my life and stole Andrew.

Annie lights candles around the room, turns off all the lights and then passes around the little cartons of food. All the girls start eating in tiny bites except for Amal, who just eats like a normal person. Annie and Eva exchange looks as if they are already monitoring how much Amal will eat.

Megan is upstairs with Carmen. Annie's parents went out to dinner so we could have privacy. When Annie's mother told her they would go out, Annie said, "Ye-ah, like duh, since someone ruined sleeping out in the tent for us."

After we eat, Annie says she's dying for a "break." We all stand up and I catch Amal's little-girl face, confused and a little anxious. I'm excited that she might not know how to smoke and hope all the other girls notice if she holds the cigarette wrong or coughs. Annie grabs a couple of flashlights and we all troop outside and sneak out to the rocks below the gazebo. Annie throws the flashlights in the center and they cross, sending beams onto Emily and Eva's legs.

I remember the first night when I went to Mulholland with the girls when everyone thought I was Annie's cousin and I felt like I had friends. I want desperately to get that feeling back, so I pull out some cigarettes that I found in an old jacket of Annie's that she gave me. I offer them around, at least participating in the group on some level. I pull out a match for Annie and she lights hers first. The other girls follow. All except for Amal. The pack sits in front of her on the ground.

"Go, ahead, Am," Annie says casually. "My parents won't be home for hours." Annie does a hair flip and then blows out two perfect smoke rings.

Amal just stares at the cigarette package on the ground, her eyes big brown saucers. Annie must think she can't see it or something because she goes, "Right there, Am."

Amal still doesn't take it, and now all the eyes turn sharply to her face. She looks scared. "I can't," she says in a tiny voice. "No, thanks."

This is better than I thought. She's an unbelievable baby in front of the whole group. I look at Annie in smug expectation. She nods to Amal. "Seriously, my parents won't be home until after midnight." She's smiling to Amal, but her eyes are ice. She's picked up that Amal's refusal to take a cigarette has nothing to do with an expectation that Annie's parents will be home. She's trying, by brute effort, to roll over it.

Amal shakes her head. "I-I can't. I'm, um, Muslim."

Annie's forehead recoils into her scalp like, What kind of weird-ass answer is that? Then she starts laughing. Leslie, Emily and Eva laugh too. I just watch.

"Good one," Annie says and nudges her with her hand still holding the cigarette. "I'm Muslim too. Where's my turban?"

A cloud slips back from the moon and I see Amal's chin quiver and a tear glistening in one eye. "I really am Muslim. Why do you think I have an Arabic name?" she whispers. "And why do you think I do the noon prayer at school?"

Annie looks confused. She never bothered to ask Amal why she needed to bow at noon. She probably just thought it was something Amal learned in the South and she was too busy being important keeping everyone out of the library.

Annie doesn't know what to do so she hits her cigarette again. Holding in the smoke buys her time. Finally, she exhales and says, "But you're from Georgia."

Emily giggles at this. Everyone else is silent. Amal looks like she wants to be anywhere but here. "I was born there but my dad and mom, they're from Egypt."

Annie's irritated. "So, then, you're not Arabian, you're Egyptian."

Amal sighs. "I'm an Egyptian and an Arab and a Muslim."

Annie's face tightens. I can tell she's furious for coming out to smoke in the first place without first making sure that Amal smokes. It's way too early for her to lose ground with her.

I look at the dirty ash growing on the cigarette in my own hand. I've learned how to smoke without coughing, but I still have to stifle my gag reflex as the smell always reminds me of the smell from her ashtrays. I knock the ash off and stare at Amal. A monstrous feeling raises its black, blubbery head from the swamp of my hatred for her. I don't want to admit the thought full-blown to my brain, but it's there, swimming in me.

Dripping over my scorn for her is the horrible acknowledgment that I admire her. Beneath her shaky, ready-to-cry face is the ability to refuse the offering of the group. A refusal I couldn't muster when on my first night out here, all I could think about was the heady feeling of finally belonging.

I resent Amal for that. Who does she think she is that she can say no to something the group has decided is cool?

I see in her eyes something that gives her confidence even more than her breasts and beautiful face do. I see parents who must hug her good night and worry when she has a cold. I feel the same raw, savage hate I do when Aunt Sarah pulls Megan onto her lap and covers her with kisses.

I expel my smoke in a harsh gasp. I wait for Annie to issue the decree that Amal is exiled. Annie must do it, because she's already staked a position regarding cigarettes since she has one in her own hand. I look for Annie's lips to turn up mockingly at the corners and her sarcastic voice to say, "Okay, *Princess*, maybe you should call Daddy to come and take you home."

Instead, she does the unthinkable. She stands up, drops her cigarette, grinds it into the dirt and wipes her hands against each other as if to cleanse them of the act in which she just participated. "Not really in the mood either," she says. "But, since Stephanie seemed to need one so badly, I figured, whatever floats her boat."

The other girls take Annie's cue and stare at me coldly. They drop their cigarettes and smash them into the earth. Without even waiting for me to get up, they all start walking back toward the house. I watch them go, still speechless, wondering how I get blamed for doing something I never even wanted to do in the first place.

• • •

Noise slaps at my sleep. I dropped off while the whispering still darted around the sleeping bags. Now there's a tiny knocking at the window and I know all the guys are here. All except for Andrew. Apparently, his dad's getting some kind of award tonight and he's out of the loop.

I'm relieved. Somehow it's one less level of pressure that I have to deal with. I even think of staying in my sleeping bag if they're all going to go outside, but then Annie whispers, "Let them in; my parents won't be here for a while."

Grudgingly, I get out of the bag and slide back up against the wall to at least get out of the middle of the room. The boys have all been drinking. I can smell it the second they walk in. Annie doesn't seem to realize it yet as she welcomes them all in with whispered giggling, telling them to be quiet so they don't wake Carmen and Megan.

The boys tumble in. JKIII is the first. While Annie goes to get the leftover Chinese food from the kitchen, he makes his way over to Amal. She's breathtaking in her white pajamas with her hair a black waterfall and her face soft and drowsy in the pale moonlight splintering in through the French doors. While everyone is bustling over the food Annie starts bringing in, JKIII starts asking Amal questions about Georgia.

The questions all seem innocent enough, but I know better. They're warm-up questions for what he really wants. I can tell by the way his eyes never leave her face except to steal down to her chest and how he seems oblivious to everything going on around them.

Amal answers his questions shyly, but seems eager to have someone to talk to who will just sit down, since a couple of the other boys are getting sort of rough at the other end of the family room.

I sit in the shadows, just watching. A little while later, after the Chinese food has been hauled out and sodas and chips are passed around, Annie comes back to the circle with the high flush she gets on her cheeks when she's in social director mode. She stops dead in her tracks a few feet away from the sleeping bags. No one else notices what she is doing, but I do. I see her mouth fall from a full flirtatious smile into a tight line of fury. Her spine gets more erect. She's staring hard at JKIII, but he's so engrossed by Amal's beauty and so involved in his drunken dissertation on the profound difference between southern women and all other women that he doesn't even see her.

It doesn't matter that Amal has, by now, discerned that JKIII is drunk and is actually leaning her head slightly away from him. It doesn't matter that she hasn't shown anything but polite interest in his attentions. Annie has seen *him* look at *her*, and none of it was with polite interest.

She gives Amal one last look of pure hatred and then walks over to the other guys in the room and tells them that they have to leave now because her parents will be home any minute. While they're stumbling to their feet, she manufactures a pretty girl smile and walks over to JKIII to say, jauntily, "You too, babe. You gotta go. My parents will kill me if you're here."

JKIII gives one last drunken, longing look at Amal and then stumbles out the door with the rest of the guys.

Everyone puts their sleeping bags back where they were. Amal falls asleep first, her beautiful face young and innocent against her pillow. I start to drift when I hear the first stirrings of Annie's new campaign, whispering through the other sleeping bags: Amal is a total slut and she can't be-lieve how hard she was hitting on JKIII.

It's open season now. The other girls, grateful that the status quo has returned, and now unburdened by the expectation to be nice to the beautiful southern outsider, relieve themselves. Eva says she saw Amal scoping JKIII out the first time she even met him. Leslie agrees, adding that it was obvious to her that Amal was just using all of them in order to hook up with him. Emily bets that if any of them went back to Amal's old school, she'd have a bad reputation there, sure enough.

Annie pulls out her phone and pulls up her Facebook. "Girls, I think it's time for a little honesty." Cruel and excited smiles light the other girls' faces. They grab their phones and I have the feeling they've done this before. I glance over Eva's shoulder to see what she's doing. She's pulled up Amal's Facebook page. Eva's fingers fly over her phone. She's leaving an anonymous message in Amal's Honesty Box. I don't have to see it to know what it says.

I mull over the indictment of Amal. A new piece of social knowledge settles itself in my brain. An exception to the rule of courting competing beauty is the emergency measure of destroying its holder with rumor. Since the girls set all the social agendas, Amal will be in exile without the group. Even Andrew won't come sniffing around her anymore. Sluts, I know, even from Catholic school, live outside the tribe.

CHAPTER FIFTEEN

Amal wakes up, oblivious to the social annihilation that happened while she slept. Since we have school, we all zip out of our sleeping bags and into various showers and then into our clothes. Carmen has laid out a full spread of food, but Annie just runs past her, annoyed that she would even think we had time to eat, so all the girls run past her too. I'm kind of hungry since I didn't eat much Chinese food last night, so I grab a bagel.

We pile into Aunt Sarah's SUV. Annie rolls her eyes when she sees my bagel and I shove it into my backpack. Then, she quickly moves on; she has bigger fish than me to fry this morning. "So, Amal, how'd you sleep?" she asks innocently. Obviously, in the time pressure of getting ready in the morning, Amal has not yet had time to check her Facebook.

Annie's in the front passenger seat. Eva, Leslie and Emily are in the middle and I am in the far back next to Amal. "Good," Amal says happily. She's settling in against her seat cushions, obviously excited about being a beautiful girl going to her expensive school with her new A-list girlfriends. She misses the sharp, mean looks that dart amongst the other girls, and if I didn't hate her so much, I'd actually feel sorry for her.

"Re-ally?" Annie says, and all the other girls start laughing under their breath.

Amal must feel like she's missing something. She looks up to hear more and to figure out what they're laughing about. No one says anything. She sort of shrugs and then just relaxes in her seat as if figuring that she's just too far back in the car to have gotten some joke.

She turns to me with interest. "So, Stephanie, how long have you been out here from Boston?"

My head jerks. Did she do that on purpose? Try to remind me of my expulsion from my own family? "A while," I say rudely. I turn my back to her and stare out the window, feeling the familiar grind in my stomach. I try to push the rage against my parents back down and focus on trying to survive the day ahead.

• • •

I suffer through math class not having the energy to follow all the formulas the teacher, Mr. Specter, is writing on the board. The only thing that keeps me from sheer madness is that Mr. Specter looks like a wizard. He has a severe comb-over of thin, dyed red hair and long yellow teeth. I'd love to leap up, stick my pencil out like a wand and yell something Harry Potterish, like, "Expelliderus!"

That would certainly give Annie, who I can see is texting madly in the back of the class, a heart attack. And it would serve her right. As soon as Aunt Sarah pulled over to the curb in the drop-off lane, she and her three fellow vipers leapt out of the car, leaving Amal and me to struggle out of the far back.

I hustled out before Amal. I didn't want to walk into school with her so I just ran off to my locker without even saying good-bye.

I saw a slice of her face as I turned to leave, and it looked hurt. I feel a splinter of guilt for leaving her like that since, if I'm honest about it, I'd have to admit that she probably never knew I liked Andrew in the first place. I shove the splinter down since I don't have time to waste on feeling guilty about a girl who is movie star beautiful and can have anything she wants in the world.

Math is getting boring again since it's not that fun to have a teacher who looks like a wizard if there's no one to tell that to and try not to laugh with. I look around the classroom and see that Annie's campaign to destroy Amal is running strong. Mean looks at Amal generate not just from Queen Anne and her subjects but from other girls residing on the outlying rings of their clique. News travels fast with instant messaging and texting. Even though it's explicitly forbidden in the school rules to use cell phones at school, it's clear none of the kids or faculty take it seriously. Girls have been receiving Annie's news flashes about Amal being a slut all morning. A subtle buzz surrounds her, a dark current of dislike. She looks confused and nervous when she watches Annie rush out of math class, just like she did in social studies, without even looking at her.

I'm already seated when Amal enters study hall. Her face flashes with hope when she sees Annie and the group.

Annie's group occupies the center table where everyone in the room has a view of them. I'm sitting at the end of their table with some filler girls between Annie, Leslie, and me. Eva and Emily sit across the table from them. I'm pretending to study my math book, trying not to care that the four of them are hunched into each other, chatting nonstop.

Amal hurries over, every quick step confirming her hope that the morning slights were because of some huge misunderstanding. There are no spots close to Annie, or the group. No effort is made by them to squeeze together to make room for one more friend. Amal stands behind Annie, waiting for her to take notice and motion her in, but Annie doesn't turn around.

Amal looks nervous again, but makes the bold move of tapping Annie on the shoulder. Annie turns away from her huddled conversation, clearly irritated, with raised eyebrows that say, EXCUSE YOU without her having to speak one word.

"Hey," Amal says hesitantly, yet with a hungry eagerness.

Annie wears the patronizing expression of a queen interrupted by a peasant. "Obviously," she releases a short little annoyed puff of air through her nose, "not any room here."

Amal reels like she's been slapped. Her whole face

cracks and her eyes blink away tears. I remember how young she really looks without her woman's body. I feel sick watching it.

She mutters, "Oh, um, um, sorry." But Annie has already turned back toward Eva, Leslie and Emily, who also wear perturbed looks in imitation of their queen.

Amal walks to an empty table in the back of study hall and opens up one of her books. She bows her head low over the book with her back to the whole world, and it's not hard to see that she's crying.

My heart tightens in my chest. It isn't fair that I feel sorry for her. I have so many things raging through me that I could use all of my time just feeling bad for myself. But I don't. Even as I try to push her out of my head and just stare at my math book, I feel her worm her way back into my thoughts. She is me sitting over there at that table all alone. Another girl sitting in another bubble of despair, just waiting for someone to pop it and find something, anything, to talk to her about.

• • •

In English class the air is even thicker around Amal as she sits in her chair looking around the room, stricken. No doubt she finally had time to sneak into her Facebook during study hall, probably to find solace from her friends at her old school, and found her Honesty Box filled with anonymous messages calling her a slut.

When Andrew walks into class he glides by her without even speaking. No big surprise. Obviously by now he's heard, like the rest of the school, that she was hitting on an older and cuter guy. Not so great for his ninth-grade ego.

When Annie walks by, Amal presses her back harder into her chair, like she's afraid to get hit by mean words, but her eyes look up, just a little, just in case study hall was just the last crazy piece of the whole morning mix-up and Annie will go back to being as friendly as she was at the pool and maybe even help her figure out who the cruel anonymous "honest" friends are. Annie doesn't even blink her way as she flicks her hair right over her head and says a loud, "Hey, dude" to Andrew, then punches him in the arm.

We're studying *Moby-Dick*, and after all the boys get finished making their obvious jokes about the title, the teacher gets down to business talking about the obsession of Ahab. She asks if any of us can think of anything we've ever wanted that we couldn't stop thinking about, couldn't stop craving. Some girl in the back whispers loudly, "Pinkberry."

Kids laugh but I don't hear them. I'm too busy with images of my own cravings blasting through my brain, striking and burning: my mom leaving—that last feeling of clutching her around the waist, trying to hold on to her—begging her, needing her, *please, please don't go*; my dad just leaking all over; the emptiness in my stomach on the plane, knowing I was left and then sent away because I wasn't lovable enough for anyone to want to be around.

Have I ever wanted anything I couldn't stop thinking about? Please.

I'm choked by the images of cravings and they don't stop. They just keep coming and searing my brain: Watching other kids in clusters, talking laughing; walking home alone, shoes scuffed, a little too tight. The feeling of first being with Annie and her friends, belonging, *belonging* like I never have in my life. Then going into that briefcase because I wanted so badly for Uncle Michael to find me special; the Coke, the sticky papers, and then, God, the look in Uncle Michael's eyes when he came into my room and the look in Annie's eyes when she heard I was the bad seed of a bar slut.

I feel like my head is going to explode.

The teacher is now saying something about the whiteness

of the whale and it just seems like hazy chatter, drifting from across the room, wisps of emptiness rolling up against my ears like pulled cotton. Nothing she says is firm enough to sink into me and stop the images. I need something to look at, something to calm me down.

My eyes skirt frantically around, whizzing like frenzied comets. They whirl past Amal, then back. Past, then back. Something about her is pulling me to her; something in the set of her head, the tilt of her jaw. It's me again, just like in study hall. She's looking around and seeing no one. She's craving too.

I follow Amal out of the class. Walking behind her I see mean looks from other kids absorb into her skin as if she had no more protection than a milky-white baby on a sundeck. Some of the looks aren't mean. They're even worse, they're blank, like the molecules in her body don't take up any space in the air and she's fading, fading into obscurity. Fading like a ghost, like I've always been. The more blank looks she gets, the lower her shoulders sag, until she's almost a letter C, walking through a gray foam of suffocating silence.

I follow her into the library and browse the shelves, pretending to look at a book while she does her noon bends and bows in the corner. When she finishes and walks toward the door, I breathe in deeply and walk up to her. "Are, um, you doing anything for lunch?"

Her little girl face looks wary. I was such a witch to her this morning, she probably thinks she can't trust me. I jump in to scatter her nervousness. "I was just going to sit outside," I say. "Away from everything."

She turns to the window. The sun bends gently, easing from the blistering beats of summer to the smooth brushings of autumn. The lawn whispers in lazy zigzags of windswept grass. Her face lets go of just the slightest bit of tension. "Okay," she says quietly.

We walk through the storm of students, getting occasional curious glances that make our eyes flicker toward each other as if, just possibly, we may have the beginnings of a secret. When we get outside, three football players rush by us and I think I hear the word *slut* in the great wash of scraping shoes, heaving bodies and inarticulate grunts. She falters and darts her eyes at me as if I could be part of an elaborate setup designed for her humiliation.

"Come on," I say rapidly. "Let's go and relax."

Amal follows me almost blindly now, hope sparking over her face in tiny lights. I stop and sit down on a wooden bench, big enough for two, where we can dangle our legs as if they were part of a flowering plant flirting with the short crew-cut of the earth below.

She opens her backpack and pulls out an ordinary protein bar. I'm thrown for a moment, disappointed. After watching her bows in the library, I expected something so fragrantly exotic that smoke would swirl around it and whisper secrets of pyramids and sphinxes into the seven winds. She puts the protein bar on her lap and looks at me. "My mom always sticks one of these in my backpack for emergencies. I figured I was going to buy..."

She leaves it hanging. We both know she'd rather fall into a nest of snakes than face the cafeteria today.

I take out the bagel, now kind of hard, that I had stuffed into my backpack after Annie's ugly look in the car this morning. Then I toss out the two Snickers bars I stole from Megan's "goody" drawer and keep for emergencies. "Want one?"

She smiles and nods. "Rule number one, never say no to chocolate."

I smile back, so glad that unlike Annie and her friends there's no mention of fat grams or carbs.

I toss her the Snickers bar. She catches it midair and grins. "Ya know, y'all talk funny and everything, but I guess y'all are all right." She speaks in as exaggerated a southern accent as she can muster.

I grossly exaggerate my Boston accent and say, "That's exactly what I neva undastood about you Confederates: one person is not 'y'all.'"

We start to laugh, then she says, "You mean, y'all aren't y'all?"

"Go sit ova thaya," I say, and we laugh again while we unwrap our Snickers bars and bite into the sweet, milky chocolate, feeling the soft sun on our backs and for me, the first easing of the tension I've felt in my shoulders in what seems like forever.

CHAPTER SIXTEEN

"She was, like, having lunch with Amal," Annie informs Leslie, Eva and Emily as soon as we get into Aunt Sarah's car.

I expected this. The outrage of the pack and the pressure to bend to its ways, even though, for all intents and purposes, I'm outside it too. The other girls stare at me and they all wait for me to deny it. I feel the force of their stares pushing into my forehead. They want to watch me twist and turn in my stumbling explanations while they cross-examine with their sharp contempt.

I think about the women I've been reading about. After Harriet Tubman, I devoured a couple more biographies. Real women who have tough jobs and stand up to pressure. Surely, if Harriet Tubman can risk her life to help people out of slavery and Sally Ride can take on outer space, I can deal with these girls.

I run my eyes slowly over all of them while they wait, like buzzards, eager to tear my face off. I say nothing, since, technically, there is no question pending.

They can't stand it that I haven't started babbling about my innocence or begged for forgiveness. The currency in their group is words. Not good words like Warrior Words, but hurting words or words to show who is on the top and who is on the bottom. They're getting desperate to put me in my place, so I say nothing.

Annie looks furious. "Well, weren't you?"

They all lean in. Vultures, waiting.

"Yes," I answer simply, eyes wide open.

Their frustration zings through the car. Who the hell do I think I am to break such a critical commandment: Thou shall not dine with the enemy of thou's superior. Especially, when thou is staying at thou's superior's house.

Annie digs in for more. "So, what did she say?"

"About what?"

"About us."

"Nothing."

Annie flits her eyes to the other girls and then stares at me, incredulous. "So are you going to have lunch with her again?"

I think about the shimmering leaves outside at lunch, the slow ripple of the grass, and the way the sun warmed my back while we ate. I feel the little seedling of self-acceptance that is starting to grow inside me. "I hope so," I answer honestly. "She's really nice."

Annie recoils hard as if I were a serpent that suddenly sprang up in her face. She's so angry that she doesn't even have a word for me. Eva comes to her rescue and says with all the venom she can summon, "Pathetic."

I adjust my head so that I can look out the window as the car glides home. I've never felt so clean in my life.

• • •

At dinner, Annie tries several different strategies with me. Suddenly, I've become a Person of Interest, like they say in cop shows. After finding out that I lied about my whole history in Boston and that I vomited all over Andrew, she pretty much wrote me off to obscurity. Now, however, I am open and notoriously rebelling against her rule.

Now it's time to take out the claws.

She starts work at dinner. Uncle Michael is out of town on business, so she's freer to control the flow of conversation since Aunt Sarah always takes a backseat to her, just like she does to her husband when he is there. Annie opens with an eager onslaught of information, informing Aunt Sarah that she thinks she has an excellent chance of making the cheerleading squad but she's worried that Leslie and Emily will not because Leslie is too fat and does not have the right attitude and Emily is too shy.

All the while she is crowing to Aunt Sarah, she sneaks glances at my face, hoping, no doubt, to see splinters of loneliness breaking through my new façade of removed serenity I adopt when I'm around her. I see her getting frustrated that she can't break into me. She liked it better when I was the exposed mollusk and wore my humiliation like a greasy membrane. She feels uncomfortable around me now. Not only am I not bowing and scraping to her dominance, and begging with lonely, haunted eyes to be part of her group, but she senses on some primitive level that incomprehensibly I may not even care.

The funny thing is that the look I put on my face is starting to actually resemble what I feel inside. For the first time in my life, there is not a great disconnect between the inside and the outside. In the past, since I was old enough to feel the sting of the outside glances, I became an expert at fixing my expressions into masks that protected the roiling turmoil inside. At my school in Boston, I strode down the halls rapidly, Determination and Purpose set in my face. A façade so strong that no one could see the geysers of despair shooting up inside me, threatening to burst through and knock people over. Where I would drop down and smother them with hungry whispers: *Please talk to me; please, please, please, just talk to me.*

When Annie gets absolutely no response from me, her face tightens in the middle of her forehead and she jabs, "I didn't even think of asking Stephanie to try out. Even if she ever made it, which, let's face it, would be a miracle, she'd never get to actually go to very many games since she's obviously not going to be here that long."

Aunt Sarah looks up, shocked and embarrassed at her

daughter's meanness. Then she feels the currents of Annie's power, emanating from her perfect blue eyes and arrogant, strong shoulders, and all she says is a halfhearted, "Annie!" Then she looks at me meekly and asks if I want more rice.

I decline and quietly just asked to be excused. I hurry upstairs to my room and take out my biography on Eleanor Roosevelt. But before I bury myself in the strength of this great woman, I stare up at the ceiling and smile, thinking of school tomorrow, of having lunch with my friend Amal.

• • •

In a weird way, I have energized Annie's little group. They have a whole new dimension to discuss and analyze now that Annie officially has an enemy living in her own home, a street urchin who has the nerve to defect from the rosy camp of insiders rather than being content to sniff at its sidelines and live off its crumbs.

I can only imagine how many things they "can't believe" about me.

At school the next day, Annie plays her trump card, right before lunch when she and the rest of the Viperess Four come up to my locker. I'm putting my books away and pulling out a lunch of a sandwich, carrot sticks and an apple that I put together this morning when everyone was up in bed.

"Stephanie," she says in what I now recognize as her classic condescending tone. "I think you owe the girls here an apology."

I wait. Her eyes are sputtering torches, needing to be lit by my insecurity and social fumbling.

I stand tranquil.

A hard sneer transforms her pretty mouth as she moves in for the kill. "I told the girls and Andrew that everything you said about Boston was a lie. That your mom is a total alcoholic who left you and that's why my family is stuck with you, because now she's in rehab or something and your dad is, like, totally pathetic and can't manage. And, of course, you're poor."

I stand and absorb, and the moment is frozen. It's like in that book by George Orwell, *1984*, when everyone has a room, 101, which holds whatever is their greatest fear in the world. This is mine. Being publicly unmasked. Stripped for all to see, right down to my ripped and faded underwear, with the elastic hanging loose.

I should be shaking and cringing and my stomach filled with the familiar eels clicking their tails and snapping at each other, but I'm not. I look at the dark, mean faces in front of me with their vampire eagerness, wanting to feast on the blood of my humiliation, and I just shudder. I shudder for the cold chambers where their hearts are supposed to be. I realize that I could be humiliated in front of them only if I held them in any respect.

"You're right," I say directly to Annie. "I do owe them an apology." I turn to face the three girls. "I'm sorry I lied to you."

Not waiting for any answer, I turn, snap my locker shut, and then take off for the library. I get there just as Amal is leaving. Her disappointed face lights up at the sight of me, like she was afraid I wouldn't be there, even though we said warm hi's in math and English this morning and walked down the hall together twice.

We automatically go out to our spot on the lawn. While we unwrap our sandwiches, I ask her if she ever noticed that Mr. Specter looks like a wizard. She almost falls over, she's laughing so hard.

"Totally," she gasps and bursts out laughing.

I laugh too, then take a carrot stick and point it at her, "Calculomus! Algebreus!"

She laughs even harder, which makes *me* laugh harder,

and a warm incredible lightness of being floats in my chest. We finish our sandwiches and she takes a small wrapped pastry from her lunch bag and hands it to me. "My mom made this for you," she says.

I pick up the pastry and stare at it. Its flaky layers of golden brown crust rise in misty rays and bend toward me. I picture a woman, a *mother,* mixing ingredients, leaning into an oven and mopping back her hair, all for me.

I nod because I'm too full to speak.

"I hope you like it," she says in a shy voice. "It's baklava. Like with honey and nuts and stuff."

I unwrap the plastic. A fragrance of unbelievable sweetness hits my nostrils. For a second I think maybe I should say that I'm not that hungry. Because maybe I'm being disloyal to my own mother if I eat this. Then, I remember that my mother left *me,* and my mouth waters for its texture and the insides of my cheeks ache for the first taste.

When my teeth finally break through the crust and into the thick mortar of honey and nuts, all guilt about hungering for a mother who isn't hungering for me is suspended. Unearthly comfort presses down on my tongue and onto the roof of my mouth. In the cave behind my lips I am lifted into another mother's embrace.

I open my eyes, not even realizing that I'd closed them. I brace myself for a blow from Amal like Annie delivered about my being in love with a cinnamon bun. Instead, she takes a bite from an identical pastry in her hand and closes her eyes. She is naked and unashamed of the pleasure on her face. She opens her eyes and smiles with our shared experience. "I knew you'd like it," she whispers.

When Amal invites me over to her house for Saturday afternoon, I don't even think before "yes" flies out of my mouth, and an unbelievable joy ripples through me, tasty and blissful, like that first bite of baklava.

CHAPTER SEVENTEEN

Excitement buzzes through Annie's house. Apparently, one of Uncle Michael's clients is a professor at the American Film Institute who likes a teenage audience to watch some of his student films before they're entered in any festivals.

So, Annie's family gets to host the Sullivan Family Film Festival in their movie theater, and Annie and her crew get to grade them. I didn't even know they had a movie theater in their house when I first got there; I thought it was like some weird extra garage or something.

Annie has sent out engraved invitations that say "black tie optional." Most of the guys have already told her that they're sticking to jeans, since it did say "optional," but all of the girls have purchased new, resplendent gowns. Annie's mom hired two makeup and hair people to come to the house to do Annie's core group. Altogether, Annie has invited thirty people and her mother has invited another thirty of her and Uncle Michael's friends.

I'm lying on my bed just trying to figure out how to tell Aunt Sarah I have the flu so that I have a legitimate excuse to stay in my room and read during the festivities when there's a knock on my door. Aunt Sarah walks in looking flushed and excited, which is how she always looks before any event that promises to showcase her daughter's beauty and popularity.

She's carrying a couple of garment bags. "I figured you probably didn't bring any of your formal wear." We avoid eye contact at the obviousness of her lie and I almost want to laugh at the sheer ridiculousness of the idea that I would own anything "formal."

I start to protest that I wasn't thinking of even going to "the event" with my flu and all when Aunt Sarah shuts me down. "Of course you'll come. Many of our friends will be here and they know you are staying with us."

So, finally she is being direct. It is clear that it would be bizarre and socially embarrassing if her friends were to find out she had some sort of miscreant guest hiding upstairs in raggedy hand-me-downs during the family's big premiere.

"Anyway," she continues matter-of-factly, "I got you a couple of dresses to choose from for tonight. Just pick one that you like. You can keep it. The others will be returned." She lays the garment bags down on the bed.

I sit up straight. I don't know how to respond. Even though she got the dresses for me to ward off any social stigma directed at her, shouldn't I still say that I know how expensive they undoubtedly are and how grateful I am? Should I thank her for all the time she must have invested in picking them out?

"Um," I start. "Thank you so much. I'm sorry you had to go to so much trouble."

"No problem at all," she says breezily, walking toward the door. "Annie and I have a personal shopper. I described you for her. She just dropped them off today. Ideally, one of them will work. Carmen will bring up a selection of shoes. I figured you for around a six or six and a half. And you're scheduled for hair and makeup at five o'clock."

She leaves in a whirl, almost knocking over Annie, who is coming in. I swallow the dread that bubbles in my throat and look up expectantly. What now?

Annie closes the door behind her. "I just wanted you to know," she says in a fake-helpful voice, "that, um, unfortunately, word has sort of gotten around about your true past, like about your mom and all, and the lies you told. So, if it makes it any easier for you, when you meet new people tonight, you don't need to bother inventing any stories about yourself. They already know the truth."

Without waiting for my response, she flounces out of the room, no doubt to deliver to her minions word that she gave me the "news."

I drop back onto the bed totally drained of any energy. It wouldn't be so bad if I had anyone to call. I think about Amal, but it's way too soon for that. I'm barely even friends with her, and to give her the whole impact of the evil of Annie, I'd have to start in with all the lies I told. Not a very good way to kick off a friendship.

I sit up again and stare at the bags on the bed. Going into this party is going to be excruciating.

I lift up the first garment bag and unzip it. Inside is a beautiful teal cocktail dress. I pull it from the bag and it flutters through the air as light as a butterfly wing. If I were going to something with Amal as my best friend, this is the dress I'd love to wear. It's almost too delicate to try on. I lay it down and then open the next three bags. Each one has a dress more beautiful than the one before.

I try them all on, putting on the deep red dress last. It's strappy with a very low-cut back. It shimmers when I walk. It's definitely a dress for an older and much more sophisticated girl. It's a dress I'm sure Aunt Sarah would never have picked for me. I have a feeling the personal shopper grabbed it without even noticing the dramatic cut of the back. Everything about it screams bad seed, although in a very expensive, bad-girl actress sort of way.

Obviously, I'll wear this dress.

I slip out of the dress and hang it up while I shower. Exactly at five, there's another little tap on my door. I open it and admit a trendy young woman named Mandy who tells me she is here to do my hair and makeup. She hands me a bunch of shoe boxes that Carmen left outside my door.

I almost tell her I don't wear makeup, then think that it wouldn't be fair to the bad-girl red dress and the people who all know the "truth" about me and my alkie mother. I sit in the white plush Sullivan robe while Mandy changes my eyelids into smoky hoods and my cheekbones into haughty ridges. She pauses at my lips and asks me if I'd like to just wear gloss. I shake my head vigorously and point to the ruby red lipstick. If I'm going to go as the dark villainess Annie and her crowd expect me to be, I don't want to disappoint anyone.

Mandy leaves and I slip on the red dress and a pair of heels. I turn and face the full-length mirror and suck in my breath. My mother looks back. Minus, of course, the boobs.

I smile grimly and leave the room. The alkie spawn is on her way. Already I can hear the guests gathering in the foyer. I consider standing at the top of the stairs, waiting for all eyes to train on me, then descending dramatically. That's only good in movies, though, when the boyfriend of the tomboy comes to call for prom and suddenly sees her all gussied up.

I turn to walk down the hall and take the back stairs. Halfway there, I stop. What am I doing, sneaking out the back? I didn't wear the bad-girl dress for nothing. Let the scandal rage. I do a one-eighty and go back to the front staircase. I stand at the top.

It's all Annie's crowd down below; her parents' friends are having cocktails on the back lawn. I wait, scanning the group. All the girls are totally decked out in very fancy dresses and high heels. The boys wear jeans and sport coats.

I spot Andrew in the crowd and immediately blush and

feel like a fool in this getup. Then I remember that he knows about all my lies and my true past. I pull *impregnable* from my trusty arsenal of Warrior Words and feel its force field settle over my skin. Here goes. The Bad Seed Cometh.

Andrew and Annie notice me at the same time and I can feel their shock like hard punches in the festive air. Annie immediately starts whispering to everyone in her orbit, and heads whip around to look. Andrew stares at me. I walk with my head held high, right through the crowd, not looking directly at anyone. I go straight into the theater and take a seat in the very back. I'm the first one in here. I was basically ordered to get dressed up to see a movie, so dressed up and at the theater I am.

After about half an hour, the other kids filter in. Several girls I don't even know look at me and giggle. The adults aren't coming in to see the films, they are just here to have dinner out on the lawn and get reviews from the kids. The theater holds fifty. Annie invited thirty. It fills up from the first row outward, as the first row is not very close to the screen, but more in the middle of the room. No one sits in my row or directly in front of me. I am an island in a shimmering scarlet dress.

The lights go out. I figure I'll sit here for a while and then slip up to my room, change into my pajamas and read more about Eleanor Roosevelt.

The movie starts. It's a poignant tale about an overbearing father and his sensitive son. Not that I'm a film critic or anything, but, ah, hasn't this type of thing been done?

Whatever. I'm going to be here only for about another ten minutes. I relax against my seat, bathed by the darkness.

There's a stirring in the air to my right. I look up in the dim light. Andrew slips into the seat next to me. He's wearing trendy jeans, an untucked shirt, and a blue blazer. "Hey," he whispers.

I turn away and stare intently at the screen.

I can feel him beside me. I can smell him. Despite everything that's happened, he still has the same effect on me. I'm pulled by the rage inside him, the dark dancers in the backs of his eyes.

I lean away from him to lessen his effect.

"Can I talk to you?" he whispers.

I jerk my head toward the film to remind him how rude he's being to the other guests and shake my head.

"Can we go outside?"

I ignore him.

"Please."

I sigh. "Fine," I whisper. "Five minutes."

He stands up and we both tiptoe out of the theater. The crush of adult voices and laughter rises from the backyard. He puts his hand on my shoulder, steering me onto the broad sweep of the front yard. As I walk, my heels dig softly into the ground, making my balance precarious. Involuntarily, I lean against him.

We get to a bench between two huge trees and I pull myself quickly away from him and stand with my arms folded across my chest. He motions for me to sit, but I remain standing.

"You look beautiful," he offers.

I steel myself. "What do you want, Andrew?" I say coldly.

"I want to get back together."

Despite my determination to make this quick, get it over with and retreat to my room, my heart jumps. "I didn't know we were 'together.'" I make my fingers into quotation marks.

I'm glad I'm dressed like my mother. It helps me be witchy.

"We both knew we were together," he says.

"And how would we both know that?" I say, enjoying being contrary. "How could we be 'together' when you never asked me out?" I learned this last bit of social protocol from listening to Annie and her friends. Apparently the way it plays is this: a guy and a girl can hook up and still not be "going out"; a girl can go to a specific location with a guy, like to a movie or something and still not be "going out." "Going out" is a state of mind of mutual understanding and is accomplished only when the guy actually says, "Will you go out with me?" and the girl says, "Yes."

"Okay, then," Andrew says. "Will you go out with me?"

I look straight at him. I know I should say no. I know I have the perfect opportunity to walk away after a cold, smart-aleck, witchy comment, but I'm suddenly thinking about my mother, coming into my room while I'm freshly bruised and crying from being hit and meekly holding out her brush. *Stephanie, may I brush your hair?*

Each time, even though I vowed I would never talk to her again, I'd fold. Within minutes, I'd break and let her stand behind me and run the brush through my hair, a caress against my scalp, even as my swollen eyes and red, puffy face looked back at me in the mirror.

“I’ll think about it,” I say, wobbly.

“Can I help persuade you?” he says. He leans forward and kisses me, light as a whisper, yet sending a blowtorch scorching throughout my entire body. Without thinking, I kiss him back, falling back into the tunnel, just like I always did with my mother.

CHAPTER EIGHTEEN

Annie's in a fury on Saturday morning. Andrew and I ran smack into Leslie as we were making our way back across the front lawn last night, and he had his arm around me. We were barely even parallel to her when she had her cell phone out, the quickest draw in the West, already frantically texting.

Now Annie is in the unenviable position of having me, an apparent enemy, both living in her home and going out with a key guy in her group. I can tell that despite the, no doubt, endless analysis with her advisers, she hasn't decided what to do.

She leaves for cheerleading practice, neither snubbing me

nor saying good-bye. Until she makes an official decision, she's trying to keep her options open.

I know I should call my father this morning and make a new demand to be sent home. But even though I have Annie as an enemy and feel acute discomfort whenever Uncle Michael walks into the room and runs his eyes over me, searching for any visible hints of something I have stolen, I secretly want to stay now.

I not only have a friend—I have a boyfriend.

I am like one of those kids from Ethiopia, with a starved and weirdly extended belly, who finally found food and is feasting, feasting, feasting, with no end in sight.

I don't call my dad and hope that he doesn't call me. For once, I am grateful for his pathetic passivity. I don't even have to shove down any feelings of rage for him this morning. I vaguely feel sorry for his lack of control over his own life. I take a minute and just let all feelings about him run up my spine and float, like smoke, out the top of my head. There's not much room for all the bad stuff inside me anymore.

Aunt Sarah's in the kitchen when I come down. It's not nearly as hard to be around her as Uncle Michael because she seems used to being pushed around by stronger-willed people who always get things their way. The inconvenience of my remaining presence is almost like just another pain-in-the-butt thing on her plate, like having to pick up the dry cleaning, or drop Annie and her friends off shopping when she'd really rather be playing tennis.

I eat a quick yogurt and ask her for permission to use Annie's old bike. She says yes automatically and doesn't even ask me where I'm going. I don't know what she's heard about my scarlet dress last night, but since she's the one who provided it, it's hardly anything she can complain about.

In half an hour I'm riding the bike past the club and up Amal's driveway. Her house is tall and white with fancy columns, like it was built by one of the guys who built stuff in ancient Greece or Rome. I walk to the front door and ring the bell. The door swings open and Amal stands there looking pretty and excited.

"I'm so glad you're here," she says.

I step into a dark green marble foyer. A beautiful thick rug of deep blues and reds lies in the middle of the marble. The marble looks cool; the rug looks warm. I want to take my shoes off and put one foot on the marble and one on the rug so I'll have the experience of cool and warm at the same time. Like drinking hot chocolate at an ice rink, only softer.

"Want something to eat?" Amal says, and we walk off the rug and into the hallway. My tennis shoes squeak. Amal's sandals flap. We're both dressed in shorts and T-shirts, and even though her family obviously has a ton of money, her outfit is not super cute or special, like the things Annie wears.

We walk a couple more steps and then I stop. On our right is a room with wall-to-wall bookshelves that stretch from the floor to a high gilded ceiling. Sliding ladders of burnished wood grace every wall. Thousands of books glimmer in hard covers of maroon, green and black, marked with gold foreign writing in delicate squiggles that I know without asking is Arabic.

I don't even remember Amal is next to me as I float into the room as slowly as Alice in Wonderland. My feet tiptoe on soft carpets as I spin around. The shelves rustle with the hidden whispers of millions of words. I walk forward and touch the bindings of the gold-lettered books. My hands hum with their secrets.

I turn to my right and see a marble fireplace with a huge tapestry above it showing millions of people walking toward a building of five pillars.

"That's Mecca," Amal's voice breaks in, and I'm startled to

remember I'm a guest in someone's house and I probably should have asked before just walking into the library without permission.

"This is mostly my dad's room. He used to be a professor before he switched to working for a company."

"It's a beautiful room," I say, still in awe, then suddenly shy and nervous, thinking that she must have a really smart dad and what if he doesn't like me?

She looks pleased with my approval of the room. We hear quick, energetic footsteps and she says, "Oh, there's my dad."

Blood rushes to my face. Did I brush my teeth after I ate that yogurt? Should I have worn lip gloss at least? I haven't met the parents of a friend since my social life ended that time Karen Fratenelli and Maggie Hogan's parents found my mom drunk after that sleepover.

I turn slowly. It's much brighter in the hall than in the library. Amal's dad stands at the edge of the dim room surrounded by light. He is darker than Amal, with short, curly black and gray hair that grows tight to his head. His hairline is high so his forehead is extra big. His eyebrows are thick and bushy. They run straight across without any arch.

Intelligence sparks off of him, kindling in the jewel-colored bindings of his books. I want him to like me, but not like I wanted Uncle Michael to like me, as if I were Nancy Drew. For the first time, I am standing before an adult, where I want him to like the "me" deep inside. The me that's not my mother but a girl who likes books the way he obviously does. I'd love to be able to have a real conversation with him about reading, but I have no idea how to make that happen, so I just stand there.

I realize that he's been wiping little oval gold glasses on his shirt and that maybe he hasn't even seen me yet. He puts on the glasses. "You must be Stephanie," he says and comes over and kisses me on both cheeks.

I hope I don't blow the pronunciation of his name. "Hi, Mr. al Ghamrawi," I say.

He speaks in a foreign accent, like a Middle Eastern accent, not a southern one. He doesn't say, "Call me Kareem," which Amal told me is his first name, like the other Californian dads would do. He just seems strong and comfortable standing there, like it's okay that he's a dad and he doesn't have to tell her friends to call him by his first name to be a good guy.

Amal grabs my arm and I follow. We hurry down the hall and into a kitchen that's bright with soft yellow walls and golden granite on the counters. A woman fusses in the sink. Her back is toward us. "Mama," Amal says.

The woman turns. Her face is beautiful and eager like Amal's, but instead of being easy and open like her daughter's, it's complicated and layered. Like each phase in her life left her with a gentle crust of special wisdom and if you just dug deep enough, you could pierce through her entire life's story.

She smiles, giving me another moment to search her face. Underneath her surface layer of eagerness is a wariness, and underneath the wariness is, in some inexplicable way, boldness and defiance. She dries her hands on a towel and says warmly, "Welcome, Stephanie."

I smile before I realize I'm smiling.

She walks toward me, holds out her arms and embraces me in a big hug.

The first thing I feel is the soft cloth of her shirt. Behind the shirt are large breasts that mush in against me. Her arms are thick and solid. Her body is a meadow, and I breathe her in so hard, I'm lightheaded.

She steps back from me, keeping her hands on my shoulders and smiling down on me. I smile back, trying not to remember that last hug I had with my own mother, when I felt the sharp cut of her chain belt against my cheek, when I clutched at her, begging her not to leave and heard the wasps buzzing inside her.

I let the memory rise out of the top of my head like steam, just like I did with the thoughts of my father this morning. I am already lighter from not working so hard to stuff things down again.

"Come and eat," Amal's mother says. Amal and I swing our butts down onto a built-in bench that is part of a bay window with a little table in it. Mrs. G. puts down bowls of what Amal says is *belila*, a wheat-berry cereal that's sort of like oatmeal with milk and raisins and cinnamon.

My nose swallows the scent. I know it's not polite to openly sniff food so I do it secretly, acting like I have an itch on my nose. I scratch my forehead with my left hand while I put the spoon under my nostrils with my right. The smell is now a hug inside me.

Amal's mother sits down right across from me. "So, Stephanie, are you going to be staying in Los Angeles long? Or going back to Boston?"

I feel a weird excitement that I obviously have been the topic of discussion between Amal and her mother. I don't even think how I should answer her before I just spit out honestly, "It's hard to say. I don't think my dad really knows what to do with me right now."

A quick look passes between Amal and her mother. I'm in shock that I said what I said. The old Stephanie would have kept up her fierce protection without even thinking. I'm torn between my old self and my new.

Too soon, too soon, too soon.

Anxiety leaps up my throat. I'm furious that I was blinded by the cinnamon and the hug. I can't possibly expose the dirt of my neediness to someone like her. She can't know I'm an unloved kid. She just can't.

I need to tell her how much my mother worries about me and concerns herself with my future. I quickly calculate that even though Annie told me "everyone knows the truth" about me, Amal is out of the way of anyone's texting traffic. I just can't let her mother know how pathetic I am.

"My mother's away on business right now," I blurt. "She really wanted me to spend some time in L.A. so I could start thinking about colleges and checking them out—like maybe Stanford or something."

Slight confusion dots Amal's mother's face. Fear sucks in my stomach. I'm frozen in a moment of elusive information and afraid I might just have erred. I go over snapshots of dialogue. Aunt Sarah did say that Michael Jr. went to Stanford, right? And it was in California, wasn't it?

I try desperately to remember conversations from Annie's dinner table. My cheeks burn hotly when I recall that Michael took a *plane* back to school, which means Stanford couldn't be in L.A.

I can cover this. "My mom thought that even though Stanford isn't in L.A., if I went there, I might come here for weekends, just for fun."

I'm talking faster than usual, and my voice is higher. "My mom was going to come out here with me so we could visit colleges together, just the two of us. She knows a lot of presidents of universities and stuff, because of her work on charities. But, right before I left, someone who works for her, on a big charity party, got sick, and well, you know, she had to stay and take care of business." I'm absolutely rambling now, my liar's words sputtering out fast and poisonous.

Amal's mom leans forward. "What kind of charity work does she do?"

I look at her hard to see if she has a sarcastic half smile like my mom would wear whenever she called my dad "Senator."

She just looks normal and interested. I take another bite of my *belila* to buy time to answer and notice that her skin is lighter than my and Amal's skin and that she has three freckles in a triangle on her forearm.

I keep staring at her arm, chewing slowly and thinking frantically. "She counsels people with prosthetic limbs," I blurt. "And, ah, skin grafts after fires."

I look up quickly to see if I'm exposed. Why did I say something so stupid? I suddenly can think of a million charities, like heart attack stuff, diabetes, cancer. Why didn't I say one of those?

She just nods, even more interested, and places a soft hand on mine. "I think I would like your mother very much," she says quietly.

I blink fast, holding back tears, because I just lied to this wonderful person, which means I'm still just the old Stephanie, covering up my dirty rotten core with fables of greatness.

• • •

I try to forget about my lies when Amal takes out a fancy bead kit that she got from a friend in Georgia that has real semiprecious stones. I'm in awe as she spills out glittering purples, reds, greens, blues and yellows.

Because she has only enough beads to make one necklace, we decide to share it, with each of us getting to wear it for a week, then switching turns. For an hour, we're deep in creative mode, trying out different orders of the beads before we finally agree on two of each gem with a big amethyst hanging from the middle in front.

We talk about maybe going into business together making jewelry and selling it to kids in Beverly Hills and getting our own label. We try a bunch of ways to combine our names and end up cracking up when we pretend-fight over choosing between "Stepham" and "Amsteph."

When the necklace is finished, it's stunning. Amal lifts it up to the light and we're silent for a moment, watching the facets sparkle. "Here," Amal says, leaning over and fastening the necklace around my neck. "You take the first week."

I'm too stunned to even speak. Talking about sharing a necklace when it was just a pile of beads was one thing. Wearing this piece of utter beauty that we forged together is another. I blink away quick tears and remember my manners. "No, you wear it first."

"Not for discussion," she says in a perfect impression of

the wizard, Mr. Specter. I fall away laughing, delirious that I have a friend, a private joke and my first piece of jewelry.

I want to tell her about Andrew, but something holds me back. If it were some guy she didn't know and I had a cute picture of him on a cool phone to show her, it'd be easy. But it's Andrew who went after her big time when she first got here. Way too weird.

I shove Andrew out of my thoughts and just try to enjoy the lightness of the moment, but the lies I told Amal's mother swim back into my head. I miss the clean feeling I felt when I was honest with Annie about having lunch with Amal. I now feel the gray arms of my old self wrapping around me and making it harder to breathe.

Amal and I go outside to her patio. The sun is weak but warm, the air cool, with a vague prick of hope in it, like smelling the approach of Christmas vacation in the middle of a test.

We randomly toss leaves into her pool.

Amal is nothing like Annie and in some ways seems even younger than me. We're now doing leaf races where we're allowed to poke our leaves with sticks to get them started, but then we can only encourage them with our voices and by waving our arms. It's really stupid and silly, but we call the leaves names like it's a big-time horse race and we crack each other up with our announcer impressions.

A clock in the house chimes five times. Amal's mother comes out to the pool and asks if I can stay for dinner.

"Um," I say with my stick mid-poke on a leaf.

"I can call your aunt," Amal's mother says, and she and Amal give me an identical smile.

"Um, I'll call her," I mutter, never having thought about whether she'd really care if I came home or not, but then figuring she'd probably get mad if I didn't because she's responsible for me.

We get up so that I can use a phone in the house. Amal jogs ahead and whispers something to her mother, then comes back to me triumphantly. "And, ask her if you can spend the night!"

I call Aunt Sarah's. Annie answers.

I don't feel like letting her acid trickle into my day, so I try to get this over with as quickly as possible. One thing's for sure, I'm not going to give up this house of shimmering warmth to make a Viper Queen happy. I walk a little away from Amal and her mother for some privacy.

"It's me," I say quietly into the phone.

"Who's calling, please," she says in her witchiest voice,

even though, of course, she knows it's me. I figure she's decided for the moment to stay enemies with me even though I'm now with Andrew.

I'm not playing. My new self is not shaky when it comes to dealing with Annie. "Just tell Aunt Sarah that I won't be home tonight. I'm sleeping over at Amal's," I say in a firm voice.

I wait for her to confirm that she'll do this, but all she says is, "But she's not really your aunt, now, is she?"

I quietly click off the phone, then turn to Amal and her mom and say brightly, "My aunt says it's fine."

CHAPTER NINETEEN

Voices rumble. Amal and I are in their piano room at the top of the stairs lying on the floor so that we can see into the foyer but no one can see us. She puts a hand over her mouth to keep from laughing. We're spying on her parents and their friends.

I look at Amal's happy face and take in the moment, like I'm feeling the pulse on my life. I appreciate that it's the same scene as with Annie, when we were hiding under the gazebo, but this time, I'm unburdened by any fear of my exposure. I can enjoy this to the fullest. I can just be a girl, hanging with her girlfriend, seeing if the grown-ups say something that we're not supposed to hear because it's supposedly too sophisticated for our delicate young ears.

Two loud men and their wives stand near the door opposite Amal's parents. Everyone is speaking Arabic. It sounds like a fight, but Amal whispers that what's going on is that her parents keep demanding that the guests stay for dinner while the guests keep insisting that they couldn't possibly impose. This goes on for fifteen minutes.

Amal says this is not unusual and it would be shockingly rude for either her parents not to fight to have the guests stay or the guests not to fight to not impose. Finally, her mother laughs and takes one of the women by the arm and everyone goes into the dining room.

They're going to eat a long grown-up meal. We already had some kind of really delicious lamb-and-rice dish in the kitchen earlier with Amal's mother.

Amal decides that we're done watching her parents. She stands up. "You want to see something hilarious?"

I nod. She turns back into their piano room, which has a huge grand piano, a gold couch with fancy wood and lots of pictures in gold frames. I follow her to the table with the pictures. She picks up an old black-and-white photo of a man with a beard and black glasses. She giggles. "This is my dad. Right after they got married."

I take the photo out of Amal's hands and really stare at his features. His eyes catch me. They are shy behind the glasses. Happy. His smile, with slightly protruding teeth, eats up the picture.

"Can you believe those glasses?" Amal asks and leans forward as if to share a big secret. "My dad was a major nerd. He came here from Egypt when he was ten. All he did was study, study, study. They met in chemistry class at Princeton. He was planning to be a professor and she was planning to be a doctor. He's older than my mom. He didn't go straight through to college.

"Anyway, my mom was supposed to marry his cousin, who was, like, really good-looking but totally arrogant. My dad serenaded my mom at her uncle's house. That's where she was living while she was in the United States."

Amal walks over to a large armoire and opens it. She pulls out a CD and puts it in the player. "Wait 'til you hear the song he sang her." She deftly pushes the correct buttons and leans back, unselfconscious and emboldened with the strength of being the custodian of cherished family lore.

I'm struck once again by the difference between her and

Annie. Annie always acts as if her parents are insufferable idiots, necessary servants to fuel her numerous material and social needs. Amal has a warmth and respect toward her parents. Like even though they may be amusing to her, because they are old-fashioned and from another era, they still had a valued life history before she was born.

Old-fashioned music slips out. A voice I recognize as Ray Charles from my dad's CDs yearns across the years. *You give your hand to me, and then you say hello and I can hardly speak, my heart is beating so, and anyone can tell, you think you know me well, but you don't know me.*

Amal and I lie on the floor, on our backs, with our heads almost touching and our feet opposite of each other in a long, unbroken line. The music swirls around us. It's a powerful song about a guy who dreams about a girl who doesn't dream about him.

The last lines pull at my heart in their pure longing: *You give your hand to me and then you say goodbye. I watch you walk away beside the lucky guy. You'll never, never know, the one who loves you so, oh, you don't know me.*

I picture Amal's dad, singing his heart out and opening up all his vulnerability to a woman who may or may not accept him.

I wonder how he could have done that. I wonder how he could have been so brave.

We have no lights on, and the sun's last rays stretch feebly across the room. We're still lying in our line.

"So, what happened?" I ask, and my voice floats up to the ceiling.

Amal sits up. "My mom said she saw my dad for the first time after he sang that song. She saw his courage and his kindness. She ended up dumping the arrogant cousin and, obviously, the rest is history."

I ponder it all. A brave man in love with a woman, making a choice to act, to have her get to know him.

I think of Andrew for a moment and what I really like about him. I feel confused and uneasy thinking that the main thing that seems to attract me is his inner rage. I shiver. I don't want to think about him now. I want to focus on the real romance of Amal's shy but brilliant and brave dad, winning a woman away from a richer and better-looking guy.

Like the rest of Amal's life, her origin is thoughtful, planned. Not random and angry like mine with two drunken strangers, sloppy sex and a suffocating marriage.

I almost jump when I realize that Amal's been speaking to me. "Huh?" I utter.

"I said do you want to, like, do a routine to it?"

I've never done a "routine" to anything, but I'll say yes to anything that involves staying in the magical heart of her family.

Amal starts the song all over and before I know it, I'm following along with her choreography, walking two steps to the right, two to the left, waving my arms over my head and then twirling.

The beauty of the love story washes over me again, and I think of brave people making choices about how to live their lives, and I wonder if maybe I can learn to be someone like that.

• • •

Amal and I snuggle down into our sleeping bags. She has twin beds in her room, but we both thought it'd be more fun on the floor, where we could talk. She tells me about a guy she used to like in Georgia and says that at first her dad wouldn't let him come over because he was in a band, but she overheard her mom say to him, "You forbid it, you make it bigger."

So then, when she wanted to have a sleepover on a school

night and her mom said no, she used her mom's own words against her and her mom just said, "Don't get smart."

I murmur in sympathy over the arbitrariness of adults. She looks at me expectantly. It's my turn to tell her about Andrew, since I'm seeing him now, or about a boy in Boston and how my parents handled his interest in me. Since there's no way I can tell her about Andrew and I don't have a story about any boy, I figure I can just make one up and tell her about a kid who wasn't from Catholic school and who burst into my school on a public school holiday and was chased out by the nuns. I can even see her laughing as I go into details about Sister Mary Catherine's Irish brogue when she hollered after him that if he didn't change his ways, he'd become a juvenile delinquent of the worst sort. I'm pretty good at that accent and I know I could pull it off.

"I've never had a boyfriend," I whisper honestly. Then I take the plunge, weirdness and all. "I'm kind of going out with Andrew."

I wait, face tight in the darkness, for her to explode with incredulity that Andrew, who she must have known liked her, could possibly like me.

But all she says is, "Tell me everything!" with normal girl excitement.

I'd like to spill the whole story to her from the beginning of my Kennedy lies right down to the moment where my life with an alkie mother was exposed to Annie as we sat down below the gazebo, to the drinking in the woods where I threw up on Andrew. Instead, I just tell her that he asked me to go out with him last night and kissed me.

"How was the kiss?"

Better than the one that made me barf. "It was fine, I guess. Nice."

"Well," she says, "all this kissing boys stuff . . ."

"Yeah?" I ask, my throat catching, thinking she might somehow be psychic and see my future as a bar slut.

"I'm not going to forbid it, because it will just make it bigger!"

We both burst out laughing. The moon leaks in through the window, merging the shadows of our sleeping bags, into one, big, cozy bed.

• • •

Amal's breath has a tiny snag at the end of it. I look over from my bed to hers, remembering that after we raided the refrigerator around two in the morning, we were so tired we decided to forgo the floor and just drop into the sturdy comfort of the beds.

Morning sunlight splinters through the cracks in her blinds. I stare in disbelief at the blood on my hands. I press my fingers together. The blood feels sticky and oily at the same time. It smells dark and earthy as if it were never meant for open air.

I want to scream but I can't.

I look wildly to see if the window is smashed behind the blinds and wonder how I could have slept through some kind of attack.

Amal murmurs and rolls from her stomach onto her side. I twist toward her. Maybe she can call an ambulance. I open my mouth but nothing comes out. I must be in shock.

I know that's true because I can't feel where my wounds are. Gingerly, I run my hands over my body, starting at my neck. There is nothing on my torso, front or back. I hope my legs weren't attacked. I don't want a crisscross mess of scars so that little kids on the beach will whimper when they see me and run for their mothers' arms.

I start to slide my hands past my hips when I feel something I've never felt before in my life. A trickle. *From inside me.*

I'm giddy with my stupidity. No one attacked me in my sleep. This is the long-awaited arrival. I've just gained entrance into the world of cramps, Midol and sanitary products.

And I've ruined the sheets of someone I hardly know.

Amal moans again, flops around and opens her eyes. "Hey," she says. "How did you sleep?"

My hands sit on top of my pubic area under the covers in the heart of the stickiness. Tough question.

Amal sits up in her bed and puts her legs over the side. "My mom said she'd make us *konafa* for breakfast. It's kind of like a Rice Krispies treat but with shredded wheat and syrup— " She notices my face and stops. "What's wrong?"

I have nowhere else to go. I'm imprisoned in this bed in my own coming-of-age evidence. "Um, Amal, I, ah, just started my period." My cheeks are already flaming red so I tell her all of it. "For the first time."

She jumps up, her eyes wide open. "Like, in the bed?"

I could die I'm so embarrassed. "I'm sorry about your sheets," I whisper. "I'll pay for everything." But she's already running toward the door.

"Don't move," she shouts over her shoulder as if I'm an accident victim, cruelly abandoned by a drunken driver.

Within seconds Amal's mother is in the room. The layers

in her face are splitting and splicing. The wariness I first saw is breaking up like cracked dirt on a sun-baked ground. Her boldness grows through it in a tulip of eagerness. She grabs my hand and kisses my forehead. "First," she says, "let's get you cleaned up."

I step out of bed, startled at the huge red spot on the front of my nightgown. She gives me a moment in the bathroom by myself and then comes in and explains the options of tampons or pads and laughs about the days when women wore belts and napkins.

After I'm put back together, she looks me in the face with strong womanly eyes and says, "This is a wonderful moment for you because the good things in your life will not change because of this moment."

I look at her totally confused.

She takes my arm and talks as we walk down to the kitchen. "When I was twelve we moved from Egypt to Saudi Arabia. My father was an engineer. He was offered a job with an oil company for a lot more money. We moved there immediately, excited by all the things we would be able to afford."

We're in the kitchen now. It's warm with cooking and scented with syrup. Amal and I swing into the booth around the little kitchen table. Her mother brings us the *konafa*.

"When we got to Saudi Arabia, I found that all the women had to wear an *abaaya*, a long black cloak, over their clothes and a *nekab*, a black veil, over their entire faces. The first week I was there, I was sick with a very high fever and not allowed to go out. Each day I stared out my window at these black, shadowy women until I was convinced they were black ghosts. I had nightmares about them forming a circle around me that got tighter and tighter until they were so close to me I thought I would suffocate in all that blackness.

"You see, in Egypt, women didn't have to wear the black. In Egypt women had jobs and drove cars.

"On the first morning after my fever broke I woke up in blood, my first menses. I was excited for this because you know, as a girl, you hear about what happens to the older girls' bodies and you want it to happen to you. My mother came into my room, and when she saw the blood, she cried. At first I didn't understand, and then she came back with a sack and took out ghost clothes for me.

"For the next three years we lived in Saudi Arabia. Every time I left the house I had to push all my color and my life into the dark clothes. I had to walk in a shroud where the sun couldn't shine and the air couldn't stir. Many times I stumbled because I couldn't see a curb or a crack in the road."

Amal's mom sits down at our table and looks at me fiercely. "But, me not seeing wasn't the worst part, do you understand? The worst thing was, no one could see *me*. When you are a ghost, you are invisible."

I choke on my *konafa*, cough and grab for my glass of juice.

Amal's mom hovers over me, concerned that a piece of food has lodged itself in the wrong area of my throat. She has no idea that she is talking about my own life.

I think of how long and how hard I tried to shape myself into someone my mother would love. How I thought if I were strong and smart, my mother could see me. But it never worked. When the fires from the bottle scorched down her throat, she never saw *me*. I was just there as wood for her fire, something to attach her flames to so they wouldn't burn her up from the inside out.

And so I became a ghost in my own home.

I don't want to be invisible anymore.

Amal's mother had to move to a country where she could take off the clothes that made her invisible. Maybe I too am moving to another country. A new country where my mother can't hurt me and I don't have to eradicate myself to survive.

I look up and meet Amal's mother's eyes. Strength from her starts to flow into me—not too fast or too hard, which would knock me down. Just little by little, making a fresh lake of truth inside me, starting to drown out all my lies so I'll never again have to worry about them springing forth and striking her in the face.

We sit for a moment quietly. Amal and I finish our *konafa*. The sun bends through the window, warming the room, and then Amal's mother says the worst possible thing. "Let's call your mother—this is a big day for her too."

I freeze. I'm back in our living room trying to hold on to her slippery red dress. The chain belt is sharp against my face. Her nail digs into me so I lose my grip. Then she's out the door. Into the car of a strange man. Through the rain, smaller and smaller, a speck on the road, then nothing.

The sweet taste of the *konafa* in my mouth turns sour. Shame scorches me. I look down at my hands with the jagged, bitten nails.

Amal's mother doesn't notice anything strange. She rises to put a pot into the sink, saying casually, "You may want to use the house phone. Sometimes we can't get the best cell reception inside."

I lift my head and stare at her broad, solid back. I dive down into the lake of truth she's poured inside me. It's chilly at first and I'm afraid I'll drown, but I keep staring at her until her strength bends toward me and I'm treading water and breathing deeply.

I press my palms onto the table and push myself up even though my body feels like it weighs two hundred pounds. I walk slowly over to stand behind her.

The water is running into the pot and she doesn't hear my footsteps. She picks up a sponge and plunges it into the soapy water, scrubbing vigorously.

Amal must think I'm weird for silently creeping up behind her mother like a stalker and says, "Steph, what's up?" just as her mother turns around.

I look straight into her liquid eyes. *Can I really do this?*

My heart pounds like thunder. Sweat pricks my hairline and a tsunami of tears rises behind my eyes.

I hold steady, digging the nails of one hand into the palm of the other.

"I can't call my mother," I say in a rough bark like there's glass in my throat. "She left me. She beat me up and then she left me."

It is all I can do to push the words out. The storm breaks. Tears pour out of my eyes and I stumble.

Amal's mother catches me before I fall, pulling me against the soft fabric of her shirt and the solid warmth of her breasts. We slide to the floor, right there in the middle of her kitchen, where she pulls me onto her lap and whispers, "It's okay" over and over, until I cry myself out and tell her all of it.

CHAPTER TWENTY

It's hot outside and I'm sweating by the time I ride back to Annie's house.

I park the bike in the garage and walk into the house. Music blasts so I know Annie's parents must not be home. I look out the French doors and into the pool. Bathing-suited bodies float, dive and run around. Drops of laughter sparkle upward, wet jewels in the sun.

The group is over. Guys, girls. I can hear the mixture of voices. I don't see Andrew but spot JKIII flying off the diving board, slicing into the cool water.

Emily comes running into the house, sees me and stops. "Hey," she says.

"Hey."

I turn and start toward the stairs and up to my room. "Wait," she says.

I turn slowly, unconsciously bracing myself.

"Um, Annie told me to ask you when you got back if you wanted to come out and join us. She said to tell you Andrew's here."

Huh, I didn't see him outside. I look at Emily and realize that her coming in was no accident. She'd probably been coming in intermittently, looking for me. She'd be the perfect emissary for Annie to send. Because of her blandness, she was always the least threatening and the least rude of the group.

The question is, Why am I suddenly being courted by the very group that threw me out on my ear?

I run my eyes over the merriment outside. I feel a little shiver run through my stomach when I see Andrew run, then dive into the pool.

"Why don't you go get your suit?" Emily invites.

I hesitate.

She takes out the big gun. "Annie said to tell you she was sorry."

I blink. The queen has bowed. It would be asking too much for her to do it in person. Emily is her diplomat, reopening the castle to me. My heart pounds. "Okay," I spit impulsively.

I run up the stairs and slip on my suit. I'm a little nervous about going back into the mix again, but Emily will have told everyone that I'll be joining them. And what if Andrew found out I was home and upstairs hiding out like a loser?

Besides, I want this.

I walk out. Andrew shoots a light spray at me as I go by. The drops land on me, sizzling, burning, like they came straight from the fire inside him. The kiss from the premiere party blasts through my body and I blush, as I always do around him. He smiles, white teeth against tan skin, knowing he has me.

There's an empty chair next to Annie. She calls me over and motions to it. It's weird since so much has happened, but maybe she has an "Old Annie" in her that she's trying to get rid of, like I am, to let a new and better "her" take over.

I swing down onto the chair. "You need lotion," she says

and tosses me a bottle. I smear it over my chest, stomach, arms and legs. When I lean back in the chair and start to put it on my cheek, she holds out a small, exquisite bottle. "Use this for your face. It's from my dermo. He handles all the stars."

Which means this must be the stuff you read about that costs five hundred dollars an ounce. I reverently take the bottle from her hand and gently squeeze two tiny dots onto my fingertips. I rub them all over my face even when I can't feel them anymore so as not to waste a speck. I nestle the bottle safely in the towel on the side of her chair.

"Thanks," I say quietly.

"No problem," the queen says with a beneficent smile.

Leslie walks in front of my chair and sits down on the end of it. "I heard you slept over at Amal's last night," she says, her voice neutral.

"Uh huh," I say, now fully reclined and dropping my lids closed.

I don't see her, but I know Eva has come to sit on the bottom of Annie's chair because I can hear her trademark bracelets jingling. Leslie continues. "You should have been here last night. We had a spa night."

I don't even have time to open my eyes to make sure she

was talking to me, because Annie jumps in. "Omigod! I have a great idea. Let's all stay overnight at the Beverly Hills Hotel next Saturday. We can get massages, hang out in those amazing robes and order room service."

Excitement whips through me. A hotel in Beverly Hills? With fat, fluffy robes that you see in movies and a Swedish woman rubbing out all the kinks in your back? And *room service*? Lounging in robes, giggling with girls while a polite guy in a uniform rolls in a cart with fragrant silver trays?

I'm afraid to say anything in case she says, "Just kidding." I just wait and slip a hand up to my cheek to pat the movie star sunscreen, certain I can feel the high-quality ingredients holding their own against the sun's harsh rays. Could the overnighter be for real?

Annie continues, her own voice escalating with excitement. "My mom will set it all up and stay in a connecting room, but the five of us can all stay in one."

Now my eyes are fully open. I am totally suffused with the old thrill of being part of the epicenter of cool. Part of Annie's chosen. Then it smashes into me.

The five of us.

My heart drops to my feet. So that's it. I haven't become more fascinating to the group because of something about me or even the fact that I'm going out with Andrew. Annie hasn't undergone introspection and decided to lead a more meaningful, kinder existence. There is no fun night in a hotel being set up to start over and really bond. I am just a pawn to leave Amal, the Big Enemy, completely out in the cold. Amal, a girl who hasn't done anything to Annie except be the recipient of her drunken boyfriend's lustful gazes.

I'm embarrassed that for one greedy second I actually considered getting back into the inner ring of hell with these girls, just for the chance to soak up some of their power.

"I don't think I can go," I say, then take a deep breath and add, "I'll probably have plans with Amal. Unless you were thinking about inviting her too."

I stare with open, innocent eyes.

Since Annie is to my side, the first person I see is Eva. She's staring at me, not with her old contempt, but with something that looks a little like envy. Like the way I felt when Amal had the guts to say no to the group about smoking.

I see Eva for the first time with something resembling compassion. How hard it must be for her to keep up with this group of glistening goddesses. Annie, who is perfect. Emily, though not the prettiest girl in the group, still with a fabulous body and a kind of sleepy appeal that makes both boys and girls like her and not be threatened by her. And even Leslie, who, while overweight, is still pretty and sexy and assertive in her sense of absolute entitlement to everything money can offer.

Poor Eva, with her horsy face and true secret love for math and science. How much of herself does she give up simply to be safe in the knowledge that she's a key part of this A-list crowd?

Eva shoots me another glance and the trail of wistfulness is still in the air when she closes up her face. I turn to Annie. Her face is open with venom. No one turns down her olive branch.

"Amal?" she asks incredulously. "Amal? The traitor who was totally hitting on my boyfriend? Like, right. Sure I'm going to have her come with us."

I feel it's not enough that I refused the offer. Here is a chance to say something that is the truth, to stick up for someone who was kind to me and can't be here to stick up for herself.

"I saw the whole thing," I say. "She was barely even talking to John. He was talking to her. She's not the least bit interested in him."

Sparks fly off of Annie in her outrage. "And I suppose you

know all of this because she's your new BFF?" She suddenly notices my necklace. Her eyes narrow in new fury. "And I suppose she gave that to you?" She says it like I cheated on her. Like we were really close until I started accepting gifts from a rival suitor and defected to a better setup. I realize that anything other than absolute blind allegiance to her is an insult of the highest order.

There's really nothing you can say to a person like that.

I stand up. "Thanks for the offer anyway," I say. I walk toward the house, aware that all of their eyes are on me. Especially Eva's, who is so afraid to look at who she is, she can't even face that she really wishes she were striding beside me, walking away from Annie, who will eventually suck out all of her blood and leave another dried-up, bled-out corpse.

• • •

The phone rings just as I'm passing through the kitchen. My dad's hollow "Steph? Are you there?" spills out of the machine and I grab the phone, out of reflex, the second I hear his voice.

"It's me," I say quietly. I walk quickly up the stairs into my bedroom and shut the door. I need to take this privately. I don't want anyone to wander in and see the mash of emotions on my face.

"I've got good news, kiddo. Your uncles and I have worked out a schedule so you can come home. You'll be switching around at their homes during the week, since I'll be working or at school most of the day. On weekends, you'll stay with me."

His voice is joyless but grimly satisfied, as if he finally figured out the damned problem with the plumbing and has, after a lot of false starts, ordered the right parts.

I have to sit down on my bed. This ramshackle plan for my return feels like a roller-coaster car, flung off its tracks and set loose in my stomach. "What, what, about Mom?" I stutter. "The rehab stuff?"

He clears his throat as if somehow, he had actually thought he could just sort of float out the whole plan without addressing this issue. "Kind of isn't going to work out," he says. "She's, ah, moved. Out of state, I think. Not sure when she's coming back."

"What?"

"Um, yeah, she thinks these rehab things are kind of Mickey Mouse. She said it wasn't really her style."

This must be where I first learned to lie. From my father.

I have no idea if he actually had a conversation with her or if she was just totally drunk every time he tried to contact her and he, obviously, inferred that she had no interest in rehab.

I don't want to ask, I fight myself not to ask, but I do anyway. "Did she say anything about me?"

He hesitates just a fraction of a second too long so that I know that whatever is going to come out is going to be a lie. "Yes, of course, she did. She asked all about you and sent her love."

The phone feels hollow in my hand. A hollow vessel for his hollow words.

"So, anyway. I was thinking we'd get you home really soon. Two weeks from today."

The deepest, unutterable sadness envelops me. I have to go back to what I was when I'm not finished finding out who I can be. I'm going to be shuffled back and forth, never belonging anywhere, especially not belonging by the side of my father who never wanted me in the first place.

"Yeah," I say weakly into the phone. "Okay."

I click off the phone and drop it onto the bed. Two weeks? I need to call Amal. I need to tell Andrew.

I can still hear cries out at the pool. I wish my room

overlooked it so I could at least try to wave down to Andrew. How can this be happening now? Just when we really got together?

His face blows into my head. Out on Annie's front lawn. Leaning over me. His eyes boring into me. Dark dancers in the backs. The absolute power of him. *Will you go out with me?* Then the kiss. Scorching.

I don't want to lose him.

Maybe we'll think of a plan to stay together. He has a powerful father, doesn't he? Didn't he just get some kind of award? Surely he'll care about his son's happiness. Phone calls could be exchanged. Important men in suits calling my father. Making it worth his while.

I could deal with staying at Annie's. I'd spend most of my time at Amal's anyway when I wasn't at school or with Andrew.

Downstairs, the blender roars into action and I hear a squeal of "Margarita time" from Annie.

Where is Andrew? He must have noticed that I went in a while ago. I consider calling Amal to give her the bad news, but that would mean having to face it myself.

Action pounds in the kitchen. Big male voices join the girls'. The blender roars again and again. The din rises. Laughter slams more frequently. JKIII shouts, "Shots for my men and horses," earning him a new round of coarse laughter.

I'd love to go downstairs, find Andrew and maybe take a walk. Maybe he'll say we should make a mad run for it if the dads can't work it out so I can stay. In books, the boys are always reckless. The girls are more practical. I'd have to look at him sadly and tell him it'd never work. That he'd be leaving too much behind and I wouldn't let his dad disinherit him. Then he'd press my hand against his lips and say that he doesn't deserve me. That no matter how much distance separates us, we'll always belong together.

I'm so close to running downstairs, but then Annie whoops in hysterical laughter and I lose my nerve. It sounds like she's smack in the middle of the kitchen and I'd have to run right into her before I got outside to find Andrew.

I'll just wait.

At least I have Eleanor Roosevelt. I pick up the book and go to sit on the little apricot love seat set daintily beneath a huge window with apricot floral drapes in my rich girl's bedroom. I curl up on the plush cushions. The sun streams through the window softened by the sheers that float down in the middle of the parted drapes.

The book is solid in my hands. It's about five hundred pages and in hardcover. Even though softcover books are easier to hold, for Eleanor, I like the feel of a hardcover book. It feels right, as if she needs a big heavy book to tell her story because she did so many big important things.

I fall into the chapters dimly aware over the next hour or two that the blender keeps buzzing and JKIII repeats his idiotic, "Shots for my men and horses" a few more times.

Suddenly, there's a knock on my door. I jerk my head up out of the book and set it down next to me. A visitor at my tower? It can only be Andrew. Finally.

I run to open the door, fantasies buzzing through me along the way. Maybe he was swimming laps or something since he'd said he was going to try out for the swim team. Maybe he had to go run home for something with his mother, then came back and asked Annie where I went and got into an argument with her when he found out she was rude to me.

I swing open the door. Andrew leans against the left side of the door frame. The stench of alcohol slaps me.

Bad registers in my body before my mind has a clear thought.

Adrenaline jolts my cells. I feel a primitive need to run but I stay planted, forcing myself to be calm despite the panic rising from a deep well in my body.

I force myself to be logical. I smell alcohol, but there is a boy who likes me standing here, not my mother.

I process everything about him, making my brain register that there is a friend here, not a foe. And he looks good. His hair is still damp and messy, curly around his head. His chest and stomach are tanned above his bathing suit. His eyes pull me in.

I try to ignore the alcohol that burns my nostrils. I'm mad at myself for not being prepared for this. Why was I so stupid to blindly assume he wasn't one of the people drinking downstairs? Especially after he'd been the one to bring beer into the woods in the first place?

I guess I'd just thought that since drinking in the woods turned out to be such a disaster, both of us had learned our lesson.

I'm frozen in place. This isn't like I pictured it at all.

"So, can I come in?" He smiles his dark, edgy smile.

I'm thrown off. My body doesn't like this. Not one bit. But my mind knows I have to tell him about what my dad said and that we have to have our discussion and clarify our future.

"Um, okay." I lead the way to the apricot love seat.

He follows me and swings down sloppily onto the dainty cushions bathed in the soft sunlight. I slide my Eleanor bio to the edge of my side of the couch and sit down gingerly next to him. I clear my throat. I might as well be direct. Maybe he didn't drink so much that his thoughts will be clouded.

I start with the most urgent stuff. "Andrew, I talked to my dad."

He closes his eyes for a moment, and I don't know if he can tell by my voice that this is really important and he wants to concentrate or he's so drunk the room is spinning.

I plow on. "He said I have to go back to Boston in two weeks." My voice breaks on the "weeks" and I swallow hard. I could use a hug right now really badly.

He opens his eyes and stares at me. "That sucks," he says.

"I know," I say in a small voice, waiting for him to get outraged at my dad and maybe make an urgent call to his dad right on the spot.

He leans toward me and puts his hand behind my head. I'm ready for the feel of my cheek against his chest in a gentle embrace when he says, "You look hot." He yanks my face toward his and kisses me clumsily on the mouth.

The smell of alcohol is overwhelming. A thousand times worse than when he first kissed me in the woods after I'd slammed down beers and was drunk myself. Now, stone cold sober, with no alcohol in my system to swim with that in his, I have nothing to buffer this horrible stench of violence that the alcohol means to me.

I want Andrew, but not like this. Not when he smells like this. This is all wrong. We have to talk about things. Resolve my deportation.

He lifts his head for air and I'm able to mumble, "Not now. Not when you've been drinking."

He breaks into a hard laugh and says, "Right."

He grabs me more firmly behind the head and grinds in another kiss. The smell and the pressure behind my head sends men on horseback pounding through my body screaming: *Run, run, run. Into the closet. Shut the door.*

I turn my head to the side and manage to gasp, "Andrew, not now."

"No, no, it's okay," he whispers. "I trust you."

It takes me a minute to know what he's talking about, and then I realize that he thinks I'm worried that he's worried that I'm going to barf on him.

I shake my head as best I can. "No, it's not that—"

But he's pulling me toward him again, big, clumsy, damp bathing suit against my leg, sweaty, smelly, smashing me against him, shoving his lips against mine.

Tears prick my eyes, but he doesn't notice.

He shifts his weight and stops kissing me for a second.

I need to get him to focus. "Andrew, I don't want to do this now. We have to think of a plan," I say urgently. "My dad says—"

He shakes his head irritably like I've started to talk about algebra. He tightens his arm around the back of my neck and his raging eyes snap into mine. "Chill out," he orders. "Just go with it while you're still here. Everyone's hooking up downstairs."

I almost choke. The beautiful balloon has sawdust inside. This is no boyfriend who's going to scheme with me so we can be together. I'm just the next event on his playbook for the night. An event that requires a partner. Any partner.

Sadness seeps through me, resonating with the cracked rubble of endless dismissals from my mother. I feel a leaden paralysis.

He locks his mouth back onto mine and reaches out a

clumsy hand to pull me around on top of him. He grabs the necklace by mistake and the string snaps. I jerk my head up in horror. The beads fly high into the air, spinning in the sunlight, shooting rays of colored brilliance around the room.

Vignettes pound into my head with every flash of the beads. My mother's face: drunk, contorted, yelling. Me: trembling, running, wetting, hiding. My mother: bangles, biceps, raging, striking. My dad: blind, passive, worthless.

I gasp for air, but the images keep coming with every flash of the beads. Amal: laughing, warm, friend. Her mother: solid, safe, cradling. Me: open, pouring, growing, light, lighter, floating.

I feel a roar inside of me starting from the bottom of my feet and blasting into my head. My body wakes as if from a deep dream.

I plant my feet on the floor and with all my might start to stand at the same time I spin to my left. I rip out of Andrew's grasp and reach out and grab Eleanor Roosevelt. The book is firm in my hands. Weighty. A Warrior Woman book filled with Warrior Words. I pull myself to my full height and point the book at him like a saber. "Get out."

Andrew rubs his hand over his eyes, a bleary-eyed sleeper

waking to a shocking sight, like seeing snow in the middle of the summer. He can't process that someone like me could stand up to someone like him.

He shoots me a look of the purest contempt. "Whatever, freak," he spits. He staggers to his feet and stumbles out the door.

I remain standing. Triumphant and strong, stunned by my own power. I'm so tall I almost scrape the ceiling. Then I notice the beads winking on the floor. I fall to my knees and start picking them up, one at a time, cradling them in my shirt, even as the tears start to fall and I know with a bottomless relief that I will never be the old me again.

CHAPTER TWENTY-ONE

On Friday, I leave school at noon with Amal. She was given a study hall on Fridays at this time because it's the Muslim time for the services at the mosque, just like Sunday is for Catholics. I feel so special that she's invited me into this private part of her world. I had Aunt Sarah sign a permission slip for me so I could leave school early today. She signed it immediately, almost forgetting I was still around since she's been so relieved to have me leaving.

Amal and I sit in the backseat of her dad's car with our heads bent toward each other while her father drives. I'm dressed just like Amal and her mom, wearing a long black skirt and a long-sleeve shirt. I have a scarf tied around my head so that no hair peeks out. The necklace, painstakingly strung back together by Amal and me, shimmers around my neck.

Her father glides the car to the curb and we all get out. The mosque is not a fancy building. It's a long rectangle with a smaller rectangle on top. It's made out of red brick with arches of bluish green tile that remind me of fish scales. There are four square white pillars in front.

Inside, the women go to the right and men go to the left. Amal and her mother motion to a shoe rack. We take off our shoes.

Amal's mom is speaking to a young woman with long black eyes and arched eyebrows in a dark, gray suit. She's really pretty and reminds me of what Cleopatra would look like if she had her bangs pulled back under a scarf and was an attorney. While they're talking, Amal grabs my arm and says, "You want to see everything?"

She takes me to a big map that I think is some kind of a joke because it has Africa smack in the middle of it and I've never seen a map like this. That seems strange. I look back harder at the map to see if I missed something. I must be blind; it's a map of the *Muslim* world. The green shows countries that are more than fifty percent Muslim. I start listing them mentally—Libya, Egypt, Turkey, Syria, Iran, Iraq—when Amal nudges me. "Look," she says.

She's pointing to a picture of a mosque in Egypt. The Muhammad Ali Mosque is big and white with lots of rounded roofs.

We enter the women's bathroom, which has a sign that says, WHILE PERFORMING WADU, PLEASE DO NOT WASH YOUR FEET IN THE SINK. USE FAUCET IN NEXT ROOM.

Amal directs me into another room. She is excited for me to share a part of her life no one else knows about. We walk over to a marble bench with four jets low on the wall. Two women with lined faces wearing long dark cloaks are washing their feet. These women look impressive, as if they could have known Moses.

"Before praying," Amal says in a low voice, "you have to wash your face, mouth, nose, hands and feet. It's okay since we just washed at home."

I nod. The way Amal acts makes me want to share a Christmas with her. I wish I had a nice family with cozy traditions so I could invite her to see our ways.

Amal and I settle in on the carpet of the women's prayer room. Lots of people sit on the floor by us. Some of the older women sit on chairs. I never knew there were so many different kinds of Muslims. Amal told me on the way over that not all Arabs are Muslim and not all Muslims are Arab. That's certainly true here. Some of the ladies are black, or I guess I should say "African American," like Aunt Sarah does. Some of them look Chinese but I don't know if they actually are Chinese or what Aunt Sarah calls "Asian."

The older women look the most like what I'd expected, with saggy skin under their eyes, lots of gold bangles and long smocks of yellow, purple and gray stripes. One girl definitely looks like a princess. She's covered in white silk and has delicate features and soft small hands.

Along one wall is a bin that contains scarves and long skirts. Two college girls in blue jeans and T-shirts grab clothes out of there and throw them on. I'm shocked they are Muslim since they look so un-Muslimy.

A man starts speaking over a microphone and it's in English. I listen and it's kind of like church except the man's voice is heavily accented. He uses *v*'s for *w*'s and says *vellfare* and *vell-being*. He also accents some words on the wrong syllables. Beyond the interesting way he speaks, nothing he says is any different from what priests say, like about being good and helping your neighbor.

After he finishes his speech in English he does it in Arabic. After that everyone stands, then bows and bends, then stands, then kneels and touches their heads to the floor, then gets back on their knees, then touches their foreheads to the floor, then stands. They do this four times. Then it's over.

Amal looks at me shyly. Her eyes tell me that this is what she has to give me after I gave her my secrets about my family and the ugliness of my breakup with Andrew last Saturday at Annie's. "Thank you," I whisper to her. "Thank you for letting me come."

Her smile spreads softly all over her face. She reaches out a hand and gently touches the necklace. "You know, we're supposed to switch every week."

My hands rush to the back of the necklace to unhook it. I hope she doesn't think I intended to keep it. If anyone's going to keep it, it should be her. They were her gems after all.

"Here," I say quickly.

She stops me. "I was actually thinking that a perfect time to exchange would be over winter break." She pauses, then says with a squeal, "When you come to visit me! My mom promised she'd work it out with your dad."

I have someone to visit. Someone who will miss me.

I throw my head back and blink away tears. I'm too full to speak as we catch up to her parents and the four of us walk out into the light.